"So I'm a distraction?"

Grayson stepped toward her, then gently tucked a strand of hair behind her ear, allowing his thumb to linger against her cheek. "The very best kind. But to do my job well, I have to be thinking clearly at all times. You and your family deserve me at my best. No matter how much I want to strip off every single article of clothing you're wearing and see the real woman underneath, the fact remains that I'm on assignment right *now*."

A shiver of delight raced along Tessa's spine and she smiled at him, a challenge forming on her lips. "That implies that there will come a time when you aren't on duty. A time when this assignment is over."

"When that time comes, Miss King, there won't be a couple of layers of denim in between us. I'll lie back and let you call all the shots." Grayson's promise caused a fluttering sensation deep within her belly. He picked up his coat and dug the keys out of his pocket. "But in the meantime, I'm in the driver's seat."

* * *

**TWIN KINGS RANCH:
A homecoming to remember...**

Dear Reader,

Coming from a large (and blended) family myself, I've always wanted to write a multigenerational series about a lovably dysfunctional family. After all, who wants to read about characters with perfect parents and perfect siblings who never disagree? That would be so unrelatable since even the most well-meaning and likable families don't always get along.

Whether they're the people you were born with or the people you choose, families can often be messy and complicated and supportive and familiar and frustrating all at the same time. One minute you love them like crazy and the next minute they're driving you up a wall. In fact, I often explain my relationship with a certain family member—who hopefully isn't reading this!—in these terms: If they needed a kidney, I would happily give them one of my own. But only if our hospital rooms were on two separate floors.

I'm just kidding! Mostly.

In *What Happens at the Ranch...*, the first book in my new Twin Kings series, I introduce the unpredictable and unique King family, who reunite at the funeral of their larger-than-life patriarch. Mistakes are made, boundaries are crossed and old wounds come back to haunt them as they forge their new paths. And for those of you who are fans of my Sugar Falls, Idaho series, you'll recognize one of my favorite characters ever—the colorful and opinionated Freckles—dispensing her sage advice along the way.

For more information on my other Special Edition books, visit my website at christyjeffries.com or chat with me on Twitter at @christyjeffries. You can also find me on Facebook and Instagram. I'd love to hear from you.

Enjoy,

Christy Jeffries

www.Facebook.com/AuthorChristyJeffries

www.Twitter.com/ChristyJeffries (@ChristyJeffries)

www.Instagram.com/Christy_Jeffries/

What Happens at the Ranch…

CHRISTY JEFFRIES

HARLEQUIN
SPECIAL
EDITION

Recycling programs
for this product may
not exist in your area.

ISBN-13: 978-1-335-40459-6

What Happens at the Ranch…

Harlequin Enterprises ULC
22 Adelaide St. West, 40th Floor
Toronto, Ontario M5H 4E3, Canada
www.Harlequin.com

Printed in U.S.A.

Christy Jeffries graduated from the University of California, Irvine, with a degree in criminology and received her Juris Doctor from California Western School of Law. But drafting court documents and working in law enforcement was merely an apprenticeship for her current career in the dynamic field of mommyhood and romance writing. She lives in Southern California with her patient husband, two energetic sons and one sassy grandmother. Follow her online at christyjeffries.com.

Visit the Author Profile page at Harlequin.com.

To specialist Jeremy Colwell, my first baby brother, who arrived to a house already filled with the bossiest and most attention-demanding siblings ever, yet still found a way to become the glue that holds us all together. I love your morning calls, your listening skills and your steel-trap memory that rivals a herd of elephants'. No matter how many nieces or nephews or in-laws get added to the mix, you always remember everyone's birthdays and anniversaries and accomplishments. And you always have the *best* family stories. I can't wait until you write a book of your own.

Chapter One

Tessa King never shied away from an army of television cameras pointed in her direction. But she'd never had to face those familiar lenses from the opposite side of her father's flag-draped casket.

Until today.

Tessa took a deep breath and inhaled the competing scents of flower arrangements and breath mints as she eyed the cheap boxes of tissue the First Congregation of Teton Ridge placed in each pew for the thousands of mourners who'd come to pay their final respects.

Of course, not everyone could fit inside the community church built long before nearby Jackson Hole,

Wyoming, had become a popular resort destination. Vice President Roper King could have had a much grander, more formal in-state funeral at the rotunda of the United States Capitol. However, Tessa's father was well-known for bucking trends and doing things his own way. That was probably why he hadn't told anyone but his wife about the pancreatic cancer diagnosis. Instead, he'd let his children and his staff think he was returning to the family ranch for a much needed vacation away from the constant demands of Washington, DC.

While small, this church was the most fitting place to hold the patriarch's final send-off. It was where all of the biggest moments in Roper's life had occurred. His baptism. His first, third and fourth marriages (the family *never* discussed wife number two). The christenings of all six of his children, whom he referred to as his late-in-life blessings. And the announcements of his campaigns to run for state senate and, later, governor of Wyoming.

Despite rising through the political ranks and becoming the vice president of the United States of America, Roper King had always remained humble. Especially when he told people that he'd taken his first breath on the Twin Kings Ranch and that's where he'd take his last.

It would've been nice if you'd told us ahead of time that you already knew the final one was coming sooner than we expected, Daddy, Tessa thought as she stared across the aisle at the rest of her family. She was supposed to be sitting in the front row with her mother and five siblings. However, the last time they'd all been to this church together was when they were young children and everyone could still fit on one of the small wooden pews. Nobody had antici pated the fact that while they'd all grown up, every- thing else in this town had remained the same. Plus, her network producers had thought it more strategic for her to sit on this side of the church, in the same camera shot as some of the most powerful leaders in the world, so she'd volunteered to relocate.

She should've told the network bigwigs to go screw themselves, but she was currently in negotia- tions for a syndicated weekly series and these kinds of opportunities didn't come around too often.

So instead of being able to lean against her mother, or even her favorite brother, Duke, for physi- cal and emotional support, Tessa was squished next to the current president of the United States. Nor- mally a distinguished woman, the president's teeth kept making a loud clicking sound every time she shifted her cough drop from one side of her mouth to the other. The president's husband, who sat beside his wife, kept adding her discarded wrappers to the ball-shaped wad of cellophane he was crinkling in his palm. Tessa would have been annoyed at their distracting sounds if she hadn't already caught the First Gentleman consoling the president with a tender hug while they'd waited in the shadows of the church's alcove before the service started. He'd been whispering to his wife that the cool menthol would help limit her sniffling and soothe her throat for the eulogy she had to deliver.

Everyone was mourning the loss of her father, not just Tessa.

Still. She had never felt so alone. She'd been nauseous since the first speaker had started his twenty-minute eulogy and there'd been several speakers since. Even though she'd had absolutely no appetite this past week, she'd gone against her better judgment and forced herself to drink one of her mom's plant-based protein smoothies this morning. Another queasy wave rolled deep in her belly.

Clearly, that smoothie had been a mistake.

There was no air movement in this old church and Tessa could feel her cheeks growing warmer with each labored breath. The wooden pews had been drenched with furniture polish in anticipation of the biggest media event Ridgecrest County had ever seen, and the silky fabric of her couture black dress caused her to slink lower and lower in her seat.

Keep it together, she commanded her aching head as she strategically propped the toe of her black pump against the hymnal shelf in an effort to angle the rest of her body into a more upright position.

Unfortunately, the speakers kept speaking, the president kept sucking on a cough drop to keep from sniffling, Tessa kept sliding lower and the cameras kept rolling.

She needed to get out of there.

Finally, a large white screen rolled down from the ceiling and a video montage began. Photos of her father flashed behind the casket as somber orchestra music played through the speakers overhead. Daddy hated orchestra music and he hated drawn-out affairs like this. Whoever was in charge of this production would've been fired from Tessa's set if they'd put together such a formulaic and frivolous piece.

But then the image on the screen changed to a picture of her father standing next to the diving board at the Twin Kings' pool. Roper King had his hands cupped around his mouth as he called out last-minute instructions to ten-year-old Tessa, who was poised on the springboard a few feet above the deep end. Even though she'd gone on to win numerous medals in diving competitions during her teen years, she still remembered the exact words he'd been saying to her in that picture.

"Don't worry about all those twists and flips, Tess. Just jump high and dive deep."

But it was the twists and the flips that had won her medals. It was also one of those particularly bad twist-and-flip combinations that had cost her a spot at the Junior National Championships. And her diving career. And so much more.

Tessa's fingertips instinctively traced the smooth

scar the surgeon had thoughtfully hidden along her hairline.

Her head began to pound as the video screen went fuzzy. She gulped, but her mouth was too dry to swallow. The walls of the church felt as if they were closing in on her and the flowers surrounding the casket seemed to be doubling in size. This time when she slid lower in the slippery pew, she hoped the ground would swallow her up.

Tessa's throat tightened. There was no way this could be happening now. She hadn't had a full-blown panic attack since that day she'd climbed back onto a springboard after her head surgery. Her rehab therapist at the time had explained that traumatic brain injury could cause anxiety, especially when faced with memories of the past event.

Her brain tried to tell her rising heart rate that she was older now. And nowhere near a diving board, let alone a swimming pool. Yet, no matter how many times Tessa's normally logical mind tried to remind her of this fact, her lungs wouldn't cooperate and she couldn't suck in enough oxygen. Just like back then, she needed to get away from the pressure of failure.

Ignoring the queasiness in her stomach and the shakiness in her knees, she rose from her seat too quickly and tripped over an extension cable as she ran down the center aisle toward the exit. If there were any murmurs from the crowd or any cameras turned in her direction, she didn't know. All she could hear was the blood pounding in her head and all she could focus on were the giant double doors ahead of her. Outside, the crisp January breeze smacked her in the face, but she didn't slow her pace. Tessa made it down the first set of steps before crashing into a man wearing a black suit and dark sunglasses.

"Be advised, one of the mares has left the corral. Appears to be Precision."

Special Agent Grayson Wyatt heard the radioed communication in his earpiece right before the church doors flung open. The Secret Service agency's Protective Intelligence Division had come up with the code names for the members of the King family, and Grayson immediately recognized this particular "mare" as the former vice president's oldest daughter—the one whose face was on TV every night appearing cool as a cucumber as she argued with her adversaries.

Tessa King's code name was Precision, a fact that immediately put Grayson on high alert because the young woman stumbling toward him appeared to be anything but precise.

When she slammed into his chest, Grayson's hands latched onto her upper arms to steady them both.

"What happened?" he barked, scanning the area behind her for any sign of chaos or a mass exodus of people that would indicate a much bigger crisis was currently underway. Yet the only person who had followed her outside was one of the agents assigned to vestibule detail.

"I can't stay here." Her words were rushed and her heavily made-up eyes blinked back her panic. "I'm gonna…" Tessa King attempted a ragged breath but couldn't seem to draw in any air. Instead, there was a low gagging sound in her throat and she heaved the contents of her stomach directly onto the concrete step to the right of his polished wingtips.

He moved to the left before a second heave, which was thankfully less productive, yet kept one hand on her trembling shoulder, trying to block the public's view from a rather indelicate situation. When it seemed as if the vomiting had subsided, he patted his empty pockets in vain, wishing he hadn't foregone the decorative handkerchief when he'd purchased his last batch of suits and ties for this assignment.

Grayson stepped in closer. "Ma'am, do you need me to help you to the restroom?"

Her pupils were dilated and glazed over, her entire body now shaking. She was either high as a kite or in the middle of a medical crisis. Possibly both.

"Ma'am. Can you hear me?"

"So dizzy," she slurred, grabbing onto the lapels of Grayson's suit jacket right as her legs gave way.

There was no time to form any sort of plan. He'd been trained to react to emergency situations—even when he wasn't sure what the emergency exactly was—and his instincts kicked into gear. Grayson easily swung the woman up into his arms. Her eyes were a bit glassy, but her lids were still open, which meant she wasn't unconscious. Yet.

"Wyatt has intercepted Precision," the team leader said over the radio, which transmitted into Grayson's earpiece. While it wasn't the same thing as hearing the words *Code 4* or *All Clear*, it was basically his team's way of communicating that he could handle the situation so that everyone else could maintain their assigned tasks.

"Hate…that…stupid…code name," the woman in his arms gasped between short breaths. Then her head fell against his shoulder as she went completely limp. Getting her medical assistance became his top priority. Unfortunately, the Emergency Response Team was on the rear side of the church building, stationed away from all the people and news crews.

A blinding flash of cameras exploded behind the temporary barricades where several officers from the uniformed division were trying to hold back a small crowd. Quickly adjusting his priorities to include both medical aid and now protective cover, Grayson rushed her to the closest car where she would be out of the line of sight.

"Take us around to the rear of the church," Grayson told the surprised driver in the front as he laid the woman on the narrow strip of carpet in the open area in the back of the car.

As the vehicle pulled forward, Grayson spoke into the microphone attached to the clear wire running behind his ear. "Be advised Precision has fainted. We are en route to the ERT staging area so the medics on scene can examine her without compromising the security of the main entrance or impeding the primary evacuation route with additional personnel."

"Roger that," the supervising agent in charge replied over the radio. "Ambulance is on standby."

There was the unmistakable sound of screeching tires as a white news van swerved in front of them, causing their tense driver to jerk the steering wheel to the right. Grayson's head thumped against the roof and one of the black silk curtains came loose from its holder over the side window. He hoped the guy driving them to safety had been trained in evasion maneuvers.

Tessa's eyes fluttered open and Grayson scanned the parking lot behind them for any additional threats while simultaneously placing his fingers on Tessa King's neck to check her pulse. The skin at the base of her collarbone was warm and softer than anything he'd touched in quite a long time.

"What happened?" she asked. Her full pink lips were slightly parted, bringing his attention back to her face—a heart-shaped face with high, rounded cheekbones that framed a perfectly straight nose. He shouldn't notice how attractive she was, but being observant was part of his job.

The other—and more important—part of his job was to ensure the safety of the First and Second families, as well as the thousands of people gathered both inside and outside of Vice President King's funeral. Keeping the scene from turning into a full-fledged spectacle made his job, as well as the jobs of all the other assets on the multiagency teams, much easier.

Tessa's breathing normalized once she'd gone unconscious, but now it threatened to resume its faster pace. She tried to lift her shoulders, but the vehicle swerved again and her elbows lost their traction.

"I asked what happened." This time her words were more of a command than a question. And in Grayson's experience, rich and powerful people like Tessa King were accustomed to having their orders followed.

Grayson couldn't afford to go into some long-winded explanation and risk losing focus of the paparazzi jockeying for position along the sidewalk. "You fainted outside the church."

"That's ridiculous," she replied, her quick breaths making her nose give a little snort.

Tessa tried to sit up again, but Grayson put a hand on her shoulder. "You better stay low until we get to the MultiAgency Command Center."

"Where?" Creases formed between her brows as she gingerly lowered her head.

He exhaled, still concerned about a possible head injury but relieved she wasn't putting up any resistance to his keeping her out of harm's way. "The place where all the federal and local agencies, like the sheriff and fire departments, come together—"

"I know *what* a MACC is," she interrupted, her eyes likely rolling upward in annoyance behind her closed lids. Of course Roper King's daughter would be well-versed on all the government acronyms. Perhaps this wasn't even the first time something like this had happened to her. "I'm asking *where* it is. As in how much longer do I need to lie here like some sort of hapless victim."

"It's in the big white staging tent set up behind the church. We'll be pulling up to it in about forty-five seconds as long as none of these dumbass reporters get in our way."

"There's already a ton of them coming up behind us," the driver said, using the rearview mirror to give Grayson a pointed look. "This thing ain't exactly built for speed, you know."

"Just keep driving," he told the older gentleman in the front seat. "If anyone gets in our way, run them over."

"Run them over?" Tessa lifted one brow. "I assume you mean the *dumbass reporters*?"

Damn. Grayson had forgotten that she was one of them.

He sighed. "Fine, *don't* run them over. Let them

get close enough to the windows so that they can get a good shot of the former vice president's daughter right after she tossed her cookies all over the front steps at her daddy's funeral."

Tessa squeezed her eyes shut again and Grayson inwardly cringed. Not because of the harshness of his words, but at the unfortunate reminder of the reason they were all there.

Roper King had been a good person and an easy assignment—up until this point. The man had been an admired patriot and deserved to be laid to rest with honor. While the jury was still out on the rest of the King family, Grayson owed it to the heavily decorated military commander, former Wyoming governor and United States vice president to prevent the memorial service from turning into a fullfledged circus.

Tessa squinted one eye open. "I thought you said I fainted?"

"You did. Right after you puked your guts out." Okay, so maybe that sounded a little worse than it was. But he needed to convey the seriousness of the situation to her.

She rolled her head to the side to get a better look at him. "Do they throw in the black sunglasses for free when you buy your footwear at Agents 'R' Us?"

"No." He allowed his eyes to lazily travel down her bare, toned legs until they came to her black suede heels. "Don't they sell functional winter shoes at Divas 'R' Us?"

A small huff escaped her lips before she gave him a dismissive glance and turned her head away, effectively reminding Grayson that he wasn't there to trade insults with Roper King's grieving daughter. Even though she'd started it.

He cleared his throat and directed his attention back to their driver. "See the barricade next to the tent? Pull straight in there. Don't worry, they'll move the barricade for you."

As soon as the vehicle entered the covered confines of the immense outdoor tent, Grayson reached for some sort of door handle, but only came up with a smooth, leather-covered panel.

"My passengers usually don't let themselves out." The driver chuckled as he shifted into Park then added, "They also don't usually do so much talking back there."

"Back where?" Tessa blinked several times before her eyes focused on the long, narrow, curtained windows framing the waiting emergency personnel outside. Grayson kept silent, hoping she'd think they were simply in the backseat of one of the fleet of armored presidential limos.

Apparently, he'd been correct in his earlier assumption. King's daughter didn't appreciate being ignored. This time, though, when she shot up to a sitting position, he didn't stop her because they were finally out of view of the news cameras.

The rear hatch opened and Grayson had never been so relieved to jump out of a car or away from a high-maintenance protective detail. He stood to the side as two medics loaded Tessa onto a gurney.

"Is all of this really necessary?" he heard her ask as he tried to concentrate on the operational radio chatter in his ear. "I'm perfectly capable of walking."

One of the paramedics strapped a blood pressure cuff on her arm as the other bobbed and weaved, using the calculated positioning of his body to politely prevent the reluctant patient from climbing off the gurney. Thank God she was *their* problem now.

"They need you back in front of the church," Grayson told the driver as he slammed the door closed. "Thanks for the lift."

As the black Cadillac pulled forward, Tessa's head whipped around and her sexy pink lips formed a little O as she gasped. When she turned to face him, her angry glare made him take another step back.

"You put me in the back of a damn hearse! What in the hell kind of special agent would put someone in the back of their own father's hearse?"

The swear words that peppered her tirade would have been bleeped out if she'd been on live television, and Grayson knew without a shadow of a doubt that his supervisor and his teammates were going to have a field day with this.

Right before he got demoted to a desk job.

Chapter Two

Tessa was sweaty, irritated—and desperately in need of a little privacy. She didn't want these strangers asking her about her medications and repositioning the oxygen mask every time she tried to remove it. She wanted a hot bath and she wanted a cold beer and she didn't care in what order.

Oh, and she wanted the dark-haired Secret Service agent who kept looking over his broad shoulder at her to go find someone else to rescue. As soon as her father had become vice president, Tessa had purposely turned down the offer of a protective detail. She'd insisted it was because the news station provided her with security if she needed it. Really, though, it was because she'd had bodyguards forced on her back in the days when her father had been governor.

It was bad enough that she'd had to suffer through remedial speech therapy for a couple of years after high school just to be able to say her own name. She'd already been several years older than everyone else in the freshman dorms when she'd finally moved to Georgetown. Having armed state troopers following her to all her college classes hadn't done her social life any favors.

Her upper lip curled in annoyance as she glared at the man who'd caused all this unnecessary attention.

And on today of all days.

Sure it sounded odd that someone who made their living as a television personality didn't like added attention, but Tessa's career was different than her personal life. One was due to recognition for her own hard work. While the other...well, the other merely came from her unearned notoriety based on her family's last name.

If she'd been anyone else, would Agent Rescue have swooped in like that? Of course not. Hotshot heroes like him probably lived for the opportunity to "save" someone famous. Someone who had the power to advance his career.

Tessa was about to ask for a copy of the preoperative report—she was well aware of how government agencies and their protective details worked—so that she could find exactly where it authorized some rogue agent to commandeer a hearse to save someone who clearly didn't need saving. But a commotion at the far end of the tent gave her pause.

"What in the hell happened to my niece!" Her uncle Rider used his barrel chest to push his way to her side.

"I'm fine," she said, her breath clouding the clear oxygen mask that had been forced on her. Tessa tore the contraption off her face. The moment anyone in her family sensed even the slightest hint of weakness, their protective instincts kicked into overdrive. And some of her relatives were much less subtle than others. The last thing she needed was her grizzly bear of an uncle drawing any more attention to the situation. "There's no need to overreact."

"Oh, I'm the one who's overreacting, young lady?" Rider lowered his bushy gray brows at her. "You ran outside with no coat as though a herd of longhorns was comin' straight for you. So what happened?"

"I just needed some fresh air," she offered, knowing full well the older man was unlikely to fall for some simplified explanation.

Tessa shoved the clear mask back on her face before her uncle could repeat his question for a third time. She couldn't answer if she couldn't talk. And it wasn't as though the paramedics could disclose any information without violating HIPAA regulations.

"This—" Rider held up the pump of the blood

pressure cuff hanging loosely on her arm "—looks a little more serious than simply needin' some fresh air."

"They're just making sure her vitals have stabilized." The annoying agent apparently wasn't bound by the same privacy restrictions as the medical personnel and his deep voice sent a tingle down the back of her spine. "Your niece most likely had a panic attack."

The tingle turned into a chill at his last two words.

Simply hearing the phrase *panic attack* made Tessa fear she'd succumb to another one. She'd almost forgotten how debilitating an episode could be. How far one could set her back.

After that disastrous dive in high school, she'd been diagnosed with traumatic brain injury and instead of going off to college with the rest of her graduating class, the next two years were spent dealing with neurological damage that affected both her vision and her speech. But with countless hours of remedial speech therapy and physical rehabilitation, she'd overcome the effects of the injury, as well as the panic attacks.

Or so she'd thought.

This was bad. She made her living speaking in front of a camera; she couldn't afford to have a setback now. Or worse, give anyone reason to think that she might have a relapse in the future—especially while she was on the air. Tessa tore the Velcro from the arm cuff before anyone could check her blood pressure, which was now way above where it needed to be.

"Seriously. It's no big deal." She tucked a loose blond strand into the tight bun at the back of her head to give her trembling fingers something to do. "I'll be perfectly fine if everyone around here would just let me have some space."

"I know you're fine, Kitten. And *you* know you're fine. But these folks have a job to do and it's not as if we're in any sorta hurry to get anywhere." Uncle Rider and her father were identical twins. Besides the determined and all-knowing stares of their deep blue eyes, though, they'd never looked anything alike to Tessa…or to most people. And they certainly didn't sound alike.

Both King men had been born and raised on the family ranch in Wyoming and both had served in Vietnam, returning home as decorated war heroes. But that was about where the similarities ended.

Roper had married his first wife during college and then married his second wife only a few years later. Both those marriages had ended in divorce, while his third marriage left him a widower at the age of thirty-nine. After a wild and reckless decade in his forties and two stints in rehab, Roper finally met the much younger Sherilee King, his fourth wife and the mother to his six children, when he was fifty-one.

Rider, on the other hand, never had any children of his own. Plus, he'd just been married once, as far as Tessa knew, and her uncle's ex-wife had been the only person to keep the peace between the equally powerful King twins.

Speaking of her uncle's ex-wife, another commotion rippled through the tent, the unmistakable scent of vanilla and extra-hold hair spray announcing her arrival.

"Aunt Freckles!" Tessa smiled at the older woman who was as different from her own mother as her uncle had been from her father. "You came."

"Of course I came, darlin'." Freckles had teased her peach-colored hair into a curly updo that defied gravity. Her heavily applied makeup didn't do much to diminish the laugh lines and creases that had taken her over eighty years to earn. She bent over to press her bright magenta-painted lips to Tessa's forehead, flashing a paramedic—and everyone else on the right side of the gurney—a view down her low-cut emerald-green dress.

Sherilee King had once described her sister-in-law as an older, bustier version of Dolly Parton, and Tessa now stifled a giggle at the accuracy of the description. When Freckles used the back of her cool hand to smooth the loose strands of hair from Tessa's flushed forehead, though, the giggle nearly turned into a sob of relief.

"Having you here makes..." she started, but

couldn't get the words past the emotion clogging her throat. Luckily, the tender expression reflected in the older woman's bright and knowing eyes meant that Tessa didn't have to say the rest aloud.

"I know, darlin'. Now, don't get my tears started or we'll both ruin our mascara and I only brought one backup set of false lashes."

Regardless of the bright spandex wardrobe and beauty pageant–inspired hairdos, everyone loved Aunt Freckles. Like the small pews inside the church, Tessa's colorful aunt would never change and just having her there made Tessa's pulse settle into a more manageable rhythm.

Finally, Tessa sat up on the rolling gurney, which was beginning to feel more like a rolling prison. "Is everyone already on their way to the graveside service?"

"Not yet," Agent Rescue said, reminding Tessa of his hovering presence.

"I didn't get a chance to thank you for saving my niece." Uncle Rider stuck out a beefy hand.

"He didn't save—" Tessa started, but Freckles pushed a plastic bottle of water against her lips.

"Here, darlin'. You should get some fluids in your system." Her aunt made sure she had a mouthful of water before turning to the man who was still wearing those ridiculous dark sunglasses. "Everyone calls me Freckles. It's a pleasure to meet you, Mr.…?"

"Special Agent Grayson Wyatt," he said, taking her aunt's age-spotted hand in his bigger tanned one.

Tessa had to gulp down the rest of her water before she audibly groaned. She didn't care how chiseled the agent's jawline was or how his dark brown hair refused to budge from its precision military hairstyle. Any man who introduced himself using his title like that took things way too seriously. Even if it was his job.

"Great." Tessa swung her poorly chosen high heels off the gurney and onto the floor. "Now that we've met the hero of the hour, can we please get to the limo?"

But before she could stand, the agent had sidestepped Rider, which was quite a maneuver considering her uncle's considerable girth, and had his hand cupped under her elbow. "Take it slow."

A warmth spread along the base of her spine, signaling that her neurological functions were still in complete working order. Despite her recent drink, her mouth suddenly felt extremely dry. Even in four-inch heels, Tessa had to tilt her head to look up into his face. He hadn't seemed so tall in the back of the hearse.

Lord, don't remind her of the hearse.

Special Agent Grayson Wyatt *had* been just as bossy back there, though. And if there was one thing Tessa had always resented, it was an overbearing man.

Make that two overbearing men and a nosy aunt, she corrected when Aunt Freckles asked, "So what in the world happened back there?"

"Here we go again." She tried to roll her eyes, but it brought on another wave of dizziness. Grayson gently slid his fingers from her elbow to her upper arm, his strong hand heating the skin underneath her thin silk sleeve.

Freckles, though, was just as unsubtle as her ex-husband. "Did you really puke before passing out in front of the church?"

"No," she said at the same time Grayson replied, "Yes."

"Are you pregnant?" her uncle asked.

"No!" This time Tessa's voice was the only one that answered, and it was louder and sharper than she'd anticipated.

"Sorry." Rider shrugged then looked at Grayson. "Tessa's younger sister once puked then fainted back when she was pregnant. It runs in the family."

Seeing one of Grayson's brows lift above his sunglasses in speculation, Tessa gritted her teeth. The last thing she needed was for that particular rumor to get started. "No, I am not pregnant. Not that it's anyone's business."

"That's a relief," Uncle Rider said, his mouth barely noticeable under his thick handlebar mustache. "I'd hate to have to break your little boyfriend's perfect little nose for leavin' you unattended in a delicate situation."

At the overt reminder of her boyfriend, a flush of embarrassment spread through Tessa and made her doubly aware of the way the agent's protective grip kept her firmly rooted to his muscular side. Up until this point, Grayson's lips had been in a straight, unyielding line. Following her uncle's threat toward the junior congressman from California, though, his mouth softened and might've even twitched with the hint of a grin.

Tessa had negotiated multimillion-dollar contracts with networks and had made grown men cry during live interviews. She wasn't going to stand by and have her health and her personal life called into question in front of a bunch of strangers.

"I'm not the least bit delicate or in need of anyone defending my honor." She snatched her coat from her aunt's arm and held up her palm when both men moved at once to assist her. "Now, if everyone will excuse me, I need to make my way to the family limos."

Grayson's smirk disappeared as quickly as it had appeared. He put two fingers to the earpiece that could've been broadcasting the University of Wyoming basketball game or the latest Taylor Swift album for all they knew. "Sorry, Miss King. The last limo just rolled out of the church driveway."

"Well, I'm not staying here." She straightened her

spine. "I'm going to the cemetery, even if I have to drive myself there in that ambulance."

Grayson mentally calculated the distance from the medical evaluation area to the parked ambulance on the other side of the staging tent. Not that he thought Tessa could outrun him in her condition, or in those sexy high heels that made her legs look like they went on for miles.

Still. He should probably keep his hand on her upper arm. Just in case she did make a run for it. Unfortunately, when he loosened his fingers, his knuckles grazed the side of her breast and a jolt of electricity shot through him.

"My truck's parked out back, Kitten." Rider King's drawl was slower and more countrified than his twin brother's had been, but just as determined. "If the medic clears you, you can ride with me and Freckles."

Grayson didn't care one way or the other who Tessa King rode with as long as someone else took responsibility for her and she was no longer his problem.

"Agent Wyatt will need to come with us, obviously." Freckles shot a pointed look at Rider before fixing an innocent gaze on Tessa. "Just in case you faint again, darlin'."

A groan of protest caught in Grayson's throat.

"Look—" Tessa took a few steps, jerking her arm away from him "—I'm totally fine."

"I know you're fine *now.*" Freckles tsked through her painted lips. "But what if you get weak again when we're walking from the truck to the cemetery? Your uncle and I are both too old and frail to carry you."

"Who you callin' frail, woma—" Rider's protest was interrupted by a sharp, bony elbow to his mid-section. He rolled his eyes before clearing his throat. "I guess my sciatica *is* actin' up a bit after being squished in those damn wooden pews for so long."

"Let's go, then." Tessa turned toward the tent exit, a woman used to having others fall in line with her every whim. Too bad her wobbly legs were getting in the way of what Grayson assumed was a normally confident strut.

The couple—who may have been old but appeared to be about as frail as a pair of four-wheel-drive tow trucks—followed her. Grayson's phone buzzed in his pocket and he checked the display screen before falling behind a few paces.

Maddie. She never called when she knew he was working unless it was an absolute emergency. And he never would have answered in the middle of a work crisis if there weren't already two missed calls from her. His heart slammed into his throat and he desperately slid his finger across the screen to answer.

"Are you okay?" Grayson tried to keep the panic

from his lowered voice as his eyes tracked the movement of everyone else in the tent. After all, he still had an unwilling detail assignment to protect.

"Yeah, I'm fine. Was that Tessa King you just swooped up in your arms on live TV?"

His voice sounded gruff, even to his own ears. "Maddie, you know I'm on duty."

"Then why'd you answer the phone?" his sister asked.

"Because I thought something might be wrong."

"You always think something is wrong, Gray."

No, he didn't. But he didn't have time to be suckered into an argument with his little sister right that second. "Listen, I'll call you back when I can."

Grayson disconnected the call as he quickened his own pace, hoping to cover his mounting frustration. Switching back into agent mode, which he'd never really left, he radioed the command center to advise his team of the change in plans and a description of the alternate vehicle. "Be advised, I'll be escorting Precision to the secondary location."

After all, protective detail included *all* members of the King family. Even the stubborn, feisty and way too beautiful ones.

"Roger that," the team leader replied over the radio. "The counter assault team is in position, so ensure that the driver adheres to the motorcade route."

Snipers and agents in tactical gear had been placed at designated locations along the road between the church and the private cemetery at Twin Kings Ranch. If Grayson planned to rely on the additional layer of long-range security, he needed to get Tessa on the move ASAP.

Normally, procedure would've required him to ride shotgun, but by the time Grayson had double-timed it to the truck to catch up, Rider was already assisting his eighty-something-year-old ex-wife into the front seat of the cab.

Instead of wasting any more time trying to play musical chairs, Grayson climbed in next to Tessa on the backseat and tried to ignore the long-distance camera lenses aimed in their direction.

"Oh, I forgot. You left your purse on the pew, darlin'." Freckles passed a black satiny clutch thing to Tessa over the headrest. "The president gave it to me after the service. Did you know she and I both went to the same boarding school? Obviously, we graduated in different years—"

"Where's my can of chewing tobacco?" Rider grumbled when he hefted himself into the driver's seat. "I need a dip."

"Suck on this instead," Freckles said, shoving a white tablet beneath the man's gray bushy mustache. "But don't bite into it. Here. You kids have one, too."

Grayson immediately regretted taking the offered peppermint that was strong enough to make his eyes water. But at least the potency of the extra-strength mints kept everyone from talking.

In fact, nobody said a word as the truck pulled onto the street and merged into the long line of pre-screened cars heading out of the small town. Thankfully, now that the public ceremony was over, most of the high-profile guests—including the president and her husband—would continue on to the airport in Jackson Hole, taking most of the news vans with them. Only family, close friends and the approved camera people from Tessa's network had been invited to the private family plot on Twin Kings Ranch where Roper King would be laid to rest.

As more and more cars peeled off for the main highway, Tessa reached into her purse and pulled out a small pink tube. She deftly applied some shiny stuff to her mouth without using a mirror, and Grayson felt a stab of envy toward the little wand that softly traced her lips.

He shifted in his seat and readjusted his sunglasses.

His phone buzzed again in his pocket. This time when he checked the screen, he ignored the inquiring text from Maddie. Responding would only encourage her to send more annoying questions that were none of her business.

When they drove by the guard shack at the entrance to the second-largest privately owned ranch in Wyoming, the posted agents nodded. As the truck passed through the log-crafted gates, Grayson remembered the first time he'd ever been to Twin

Kings. Roper King had paid out of pocket to have all fifty-thousand-plus acres of the ranch reinforced by the Technical Security Division. Despite the added electrical fencing, infrared cameras and bulletproof glass, the property was absurdly beautiful and surprisingly efficient and well run.

After half a mile down a tree-lined driveway, the twelve-thousand-square-foot main house sat on a grassy knoll framed by the famous Teton mountain range in the distance. The stables and barn, on the other side of the driveway, were equally as imposing. Or, at least, they were to someone like him who'd grown up in a tiny subdivision outside Baltimore.

They passed the trail that led to numerous outbuildings such as the cookhouse, the corrals and a pair of matching bunkhouses—one to house the cowboys and one to house the special agents on duty—that seemed to be purposely hidden from view of the main house. It was as though the wealthy occupants didn't appreciate the reminder that they had to share their vast property holdings with the hired help.

Since Grayson had been briefed by the same advance logistics teams every time he'd flown out here on Air Force Two, he knew there were dozens of agents in all-terrain vehicles stationed along the perimeter, also trying to remain out of sight.

It took another mile to wind up onto the snow-covered ridge that held several gravestones and an amazing view of the Snake River. Cars were already parked behind the hearse, and, due to the narrowness of the recently plowed dirt road usually only accessed by horse or ATV, Rider pulled the passenger side of his truck right against the fence line.

Grayson hopped out of the backseat and immediately scanned the area around him for potential threats before reaching to assist Tessa.

"I can do it," she muttered, ignoring his hand as she awkwardly shimmied herself across the leather bench seat. The motion caused the hem of her black cashmere coat to slide up her legs, giving him a glimpse of the toned muscles of her outer thigh. He took a step back and resisted the urge to loosen his suddenly tight necktie.

But not before she caught him looking.

A charming shade of pink made its way up her cheeks as she tried to adjust her dress over her exposed thigh. Unfortunately, she was so preoccupied with her modesty that her high heel missed the side step outside the door and she practically tumbled into Grayson's arms.

This time, though, instead of grabbing her upper arms to steady her, Grayson's hands landed on either side of her narrow waist. Tessa's surprised *oomph* came out in a rush of air and he could smell traces of mint on her breath. She tried to pull away, but he held her in place.

"Take a second and get your footing," he commanded, knowing better than to ask if she was okay or otherwise imply that the mighty and fearless Tessa King needed any sort of assistance.

She stared into his eyes—their faces separated by mere inches—and instead of arguing, she took several deep breaths. Beneath his palms, he felt the muscles below her rib cage contract and expand until they finally relaxed.

"Sorry about that." Her apology caught Grayson by surprise; up until now, she hadn't offered him so much as a "thank you" for rescuing her earlier. "I haven't been home in so long, I forgot how impossible it would be to walk around the ranch in these stupid heels. Especially during winter."

"No worries," he said, trying not to think about how great her legs looked in those stupid—but extremely sexy—heels. If talking about shoes kept her from hyperventilating, he would just have to deal with it.

"Please tell me the cameras didn't catch me nearly falling."

Grayson jutted his chin toward the flag-draped coffin being placed over the freshly dug grave. "Nope, they're pretty much focused on where they need to be."

"Oh God." She sucked in a shallow breath as her eyes followed his. A shudder ran through her body, revealing the emotion she was clearly fighting to hide. "Getting through this might be a bit harder than I'd first thought it'd be."

Grayson had a feeling she was no longer talking about navigating the terrain in her stilettos. Her aunt and uncle had already moved toward the small crowd of people standing near the piles of lavish floral arrangements, leaving him on his own to talk her down before she had another panic attack.

"Take a deep breath in through your nose," he instructed then demonstrated. Grayson used to do the same demonstration for his anxious mom whenever she'd paced the hospital waiting rooms, working herself up as she waited for his little sister to come out of surgery. "Now out through your mouth."

His fingers were still splayed around Tessa's waist and her hands had latched onto his forearms. He didn't want to point out that if any of the cameras turned in their direction, the tabloids would have a field day with the image. That would only get her more amped up.

Tessa's uncle had mentioned a boyfriend. Where the hell was that guy? Why wasn't *he* taking care of her? As soon as the thought went through Grayson's mind, the muscles in his shoulders coiled and something primal surged through his nerve endings.

"I think I'm okay now," she finally said as the minister began reading from an open book.

There were several rows of chairs set under a canopy for the family. He jerked his head in that direction. "Do you want me to walk you over to your seat?"

"Actually, do you mind if we just stand over here?" She gestured to a nearby copse of trees.

We.

A shiver went down the back of his neck. *We* meant team. While Grayson didn't mind being part of a tactical team or a sports team or even a math team—eighth grade state champions, thank you very much—he didn't want anyone getting the idea that he was somehow paired up with Tessa King. It was too chummy, almost too intimate. He was supposed to watch over the family—not get personally involved with one of them.

Unfortunately, by the way she kept her arm looped tightly through his as they stood off to the side of the rutted dirt road, they appeared to be much more than a *we.*

Chapter Three

Tessa remained numb throughout the entire grave-side service. Tears might have trickled down her face when the uniformed soldiers handed her mother the folded flag, but Tessa didn't feel them. And, really, if she were being honest, feeling nothing was so much better than the slew of sensations that had ricocheted and rioted inside her during the church ceremony.

In fact, she'd only flinched when that first rifle blast went off during the twenty-one-gun salute. Luckily, the solid frame of the Secret Service agent wedged against her side prevented her from faltering.

Feeling the weight of everyone's curious stares—most probably sympathetic, though some were blatantly curious—she leaned closer to Grayson and whispered, "I don't suppose you have an extra pair of sunglasses on you?"

He reached up with his free hand and slowly removed the black plastic frames from his face. Tessa swallowed. His eyes were a startling shade of silvery gray and held both a hardness as well as a trace of tenderness. He gently slid the sunglasses onto her face and the dark lenses made her rethink her initial assessment of his earlier high-handedness in her so-called "rescue."

The borrowed sunglasses gave her a feeling of strength, almost like a cloak of invisibility, as she reached down and cupped a cold, damp handful of dirt. For the past two days, Tessa hadn't been able to wrap her head around the fact that she would never see her father again. Staring at the gaping hole in the earth, the finality of it hit her and her empty stomach coiled into a hard knot.

Her dad's arms would no longer wrap her into one of his famous bear hugs. He'd never pour coffee into his favorite mug, the one she'd painted for him that read My Dad Is My Hero. His booming voice would no longer tell her to jump high and dive deep.

This was it. He wasn't coming back.

Tessa's mouth moved as she spoke, but her throat was too raw to say the words out loud. *Goodbye, Daddy.*

She gave one last glance at her father's casket before her brain was finally able to send a signal down through her legs, forcing one foot in front of the other. She'd somehow managed to make it several yards before feeling an unexpected tug on her right arm and a concerned whisper near her ear. "There you are, sweetheart!"

The startled expression that crossed her face didn't come from seeing her boyfriend suddenly appear at her side. She'd walked into the church with Davis Townsend earlier today, before they'd been directed to their assigned seats, and he'd insisted on wedging himself into the pew behind her. In the back of her mind, she'd known he would be at the cemetery. Rather, Tessa's surprise arose from the fact that her left arm was still firmly locked against Grayson Wyatt's side.

The Secret Service agent had taken his protective duties seriously and she'd been so caught up in her own grief, she'd barely noticed that he'd been practically holding her up this entire time. And he didn't seem inclined to release his steadying hold just yet. In fact, his shoulder brushed in front of hers as he pulled her in closer, as though shielding her from a perceived threat.

"Davis," she managed to say, too exhausted to force a smile toward the man she'd been dating for nearly two years. The man her siblings and uncle obnoxiously referred to as Congressman Smooth. "Have you been here the whole time?"

"Of course I have, sweetheart. I rode here in the limo with Duke and Tom." Davis glanced at Agent Wyatt before his pale blue eyes dipped to Tessa and Grayson's joined arms. "Per protocol."

A camera shutter went off somewhere behind Tessa and her left leg buckled.

"I've got you." Grayson's stiff forearm kept her from going down. "Just keep walking. We're almost to the truck."

Davis, who was just as much a pro in front of the lens as Tessa, wiped the concern from his expression and pasted his famous campaign smile onto his face. His teeth barely moved as he lowered his voice and asked Grayson, "Is she drunk?"

"No, *she's* not drunk," Tessa answered for herself. She hated it when anyone, especially men or doctors, talked about her as though she wasn't there. Temporarily losing the ability to speak after a traumatic brain injury tended to do that to a person. "*She* just laid her father to rest and her eyes are full of tears and she is about to throw these ridiculous four-inch high heels into the nearest ravine."

"Okay, well it seems as though you're in good hands with Mr.…uh…?"

"Agent Wyatt," Grayson offered, this time not bothering with a handshake. Probably because his right arm was otherwise occupied bearing half the weight of Tessa's one-twenty-pound frame.

"Right. So then I'll just see you back at the house."

Davis moved in to kiss her cheek, but ended up knocking the oversize sunglasses askew. Tessa could only imagine how silly she looked in the sporty, mannish frames, but she wasn't quite ready to return them yet. Wearing them felt as though she was hiding in plain sight.

"You ridin' back with us, Congressman?" Uncle Rider asked Davis as he and Freckles came up behind them.

"No, sir." Davis cleared his throat and his smile returned. Had his teeth always been that white? "I appreciate the offer, but my understanding is that I'm assigned to family limo number two. Per protocol. I'll see everyone there."

"We have a protocol now?" Rider didn't bother lowering his gruff voice as Davis walked away, waving at someone in the distance. "That's his excuse for ditchin' his girlfriend in her time of need?"

The irony of being an expert political analyst and the daughter of a career politician was that most of her family avoided politics altogether and had no desire to ever hold an elected office. Her mother had been the only person who'd been supportive of Tessa's relationship with the up-and-coming congressman. Even her father had advised her to take things slow, which was why she still hadn't given Davis an answer after he'd proposed last month.

"He means his press secretary organized it," Tessa explained through the headache now pounding against her temples. "You know how things work in our world. Our schedules are so packed and our roles are so complex, things run more smoothly when every event is outlined and every detail planned. Besides, it's not exactly my 'time of need.'"

The disbelieving tilt of Grayson's head drew her eyes to his. His icy stare turned to a steely gunmetal gray—probably the same color as the service weapon likely hidden somewhere underneath his suit jacket. "Could've fooled me."

A shiver traveled down the base of Tessa's neck all the way to her toes. If he kept looking at her like that, no pair of sunglasses in the world would be able to hide the effect his nearness was having on her.

Grayson studied his reflection over the sink in the men's room at the bunkhouse later that evening. Most of the funeral guests had left the ranch a few hours ago and, technically, his team was now off duty. He'd originally been assigned to watch the outer perimeter of the house, but SAIC Simon, the supervising agent in charge, had switched him with Agent Franks. For some unknown reason, Grayson had been forced to stay inside the main house, watching the comings and goings of the guests from the safety of the richly decorated living room.

Oh, who was he kidding? Grayson knew exactly why his assignment had been swapped. The Secret Service always had a security plan *and* an alternate security plan for when something went wrong. Not that anything had gone wrong, exactly. At least, nothing that would cause the supervisor to reassess the placement of the agents.

That meant someone from the King family had specifically requested Grayson be stationed inside. But who?

He knew it hadn't been Tessa since he'd pretty much been within earshot of her since she'd fainted in his arms back at the church. Not to mention, she'd practically ignored him once she was within the safe confines of the plush family palace disguised to look like a ranch house. In fact, he was pretty sure she would've preferred he hadn't been there at all.

The good news was that the remainder of his shift had been uneventful if he didn't count that little skirmish between Tessa's mom and her aunt Freckles over a tray of ham biscuits. Or that annoying dipstick, Davis Townsend, taking a call from his press secretary right in the middle of Rider King's toast to his deceased twin. Tessa's brother Duke had looked ready to peel off his Navy uniform jacket with all those shiny medals and throw blows with the congressman.

Aw, hell.

Grayson gripped the edge of the counter so tightly his knuckles turned white. When had he stopped thinking of the King family in terms of their assigned code names and started thinking of them as

Tessa's relatives? Probably from the second he'd held her against him at the cemetery, staring into her soft blue eyes and breathing in sync with her.

Thankfully, though, the assignment was now over. Or, at least, his portion of it. Even sleeping in this custom-built bunkhouse, which was decorated almost as lavishly as a suite of rooms at a five-star hotel, put Grayson on edge.

Rumor had it Roper King had designed the well-equipped building at his own cost because he wanted the security teams protecting him to feel as if they were at home, too—even when they were hundreds of miles away from their own families. The funny thing was, Grayson would've been much more comfortable with a rucksack and a standard-issue cot out in the middle of some jungle than he was here. While the former vice president had liked to ensure his security teams were comfortable and lacked for nothing, this place was way fancier than the furnished studio apartment Grayson had rented in DC.

And when things were fancy, they were usually a lot less welcoming. Case in point: Tessa King.

At least things had gotten easier as the night had worn on. Surrounded by her family with no cameras around, Tessa had seemed stronger tonight, or at least less fragile. Still, Grayson had remained in the background until the catering crew and very last guest had left, just in case she needed him again. Not that she'd needed *him* specifically in the first place.

He ducked his mouth toward the cold water coming from the faucet and gulped. The water out here in Wyoming always tasted better than anything bottled and sold in the expensive gourmet markets in DC. Using one of the plush hotel-style towels to wipe his face, Grayson reminded himself that any agent would've reacted the same way as he had today and Tessa would have just as easily clung to *that* person for support.

He wasn't special.

In fact, the only reason he'd even been assigned as an agent of "*The Shift*," which was what they called those working the first line of defense in the presidential inner bubble, was that Roper King had personally requested him a few months ago. After ten years of being part of an elite sniper unit with the Marine Corps, and then another three as a sniper for the Secret Service's Counter Assault Team, Grayson was still trying to convince himself that the assignment would be worth it since all the extra overtime pay from the protective detail would help with some of Maddie's medical bills.

But now that the vice president would be replaced with the Speaker of the House, who already had her own detail, many agents were putting in their change-of-duty papers. Grayson just needed to get through this final debriefing session before he followed suit.

He slowly ambled out of the bathroom, not looking forward to the ball-busting, good-natured ribbing that would likely take place around the big table outside the bunkhouse kitchen. Several of his teammates were already smirking over their shoulders in his direction as they hunkered around a laptop screen.

"You see this, Wyatt?" Agent Lopez held up her smartphone.

"See what?" Grayson asked as he headed toward his own bunk, not the least bit interested in whatever video was playing on that laptop or on Lopez's phone.

"They're calling you 'the Bodyguard,'" Agent Doherty said in his strong Boston accent. "Not very original, if you ask me."

"Just be glad they're not calling you the 'Hearse Commando,'" Lopez said, getting a round of chuckles.

They? Who was "they"?

A knot of dread formed in Grayson's belly as he stepped closer to the compact screen.

Aw, hell.

The video of Grayson sweeping Tessa into his arms admittedly played out as more dramatic than it really had been. Not that he could explain that to the million-plus viewers who'd already watched the online video. His eyes blinked at the steadily increasing number of views in the bottom left corner of the screen.

"Aw, hell," he said aloud this time, pinching the bridge of his nose.

"You know the rules, Prince Charming." Franks, who'd returned from his shift on perimeter duty, smacked Grayson on the back. "You make the news, you buy the team a round of beers."

"Trust me—" Grayson shook his head "—there was nothing princely or charming about that extraction. The woman passed out and I happened to be in the wrong place at the wrong time. Any first responder would've reacted the same way."

"She doesn't look passed out." Doherty pointed to Tessa's open eyes. "In fact, she looks downright breathless."

That's right. She'd still been conscious when he'd lifted her, her lids slowly lowering as she'd tucked her face against his shoulder. Only *he* knew the truth—that she'd been in the middle of a panic attack and would've collapsed into a heap if it hadn't been for him. Grayson made a dismissive sound. "Pfftt. Breathless? You've been reading too many romance novels, Doh-boy."

"Don't knock 'em," the muscular Irish kid from Southie replied, not at all insulted by the nickname.

"What about *this* video?" Lopez clicked on another link that showed a five-second clip of Tessa pasted against Grayson's side at the funeral. When her boyfriend approached, Tessa had drawn even closer to Grayson. The caption underneath read Tessa King Throws Over Congressman for Her Bodyguard.

A chorus of snickers and taunts rang out in the bunkhouse. Grayson slammed the top of the laptop closed. "Time to debrief then hit the sack. We're wheels up at oh six hundred."

The videos were just a flash in the pan, he told himself—fifteen minutes of fame and all that. The media would lose interest as soon as some other famous celebrity got married, or divorced, or arrested. After the protective detail officially ended tomorrow, he'd never have to see Tessa King again.

At least that's what Grayson thought when his head hit the pillow that night. But when he woke up at dawn, his supervisor was standing between the rows of bunks.

"Change of plans, Delta and Echo teams," SAIC Simon said before the foggy remnants of sleep left Grayson's brain. "Everyone meet in the conference room in five minutes."

Grayson barely had time to pull a T-shirt over his head, let alone grab a cup of coffee on his way to the soundproof building attached to the bunkhouse.

As soon as everyone was in their seats, Simon uncapped a marker and drew a line down a dry-erase board.

"We've got two new situations this morning. Number one." He wrote the word *Pollywog* on the left side of the board then used the marker to tap on the code name for the youngest King offspring. "Seems as though little Mitchell King Junior had a bit too much to drink last night with the sixteen-year-old daughter of one of the county deputies. While getting handcuffed by said deputy for a drunk and disorderly, MJ decided to fight back and racked up a resisting arrest charge."

Lopez groaned. "Who was assigned to tail him?"

"Echo Team. It's not the first time some eighteen-year-old ditched his protective detail, and it probably won't be the last. But we want to finish our investigation into the matter before the media gets wind of it. That leads me to situation number two." Simon turned back to the board and wrote the code name *Precision* before turning to Grayson. "Seems your little romantic rescue routine yesterday got Tessa King into a whole heap of hot water with her cronies at the press."

"It wasn't a romantic rescue, sir." Grayson sat straighter in the expensive leather chair. "I explained that in our debrief session last night."

"I know you did, Wyatt. But that was before the photo of you ever so delicately sliding your sunglasses onto Miss King's nose blew up on social media."

Grayson ran a hand through his hair. *Damn.* He wished he'd taken those sunglasses back from her yesterday so that he could hide the frustration filling his eyes right this second.

"It wasn't like that," Grayson insisted for what had to be the thousandth time. There'd been nothing romantic between him and Tessa yesterday in the least. Sure, she was attractive, with perfectly arranged blond curls and those soft pink lips and that pulse point right where her collarbones came together in the shape of a little heart—

Whoa. He had to stop his thoughts there—before he began remembering how attractive she was from the neck down.

Someone made a wolf whistle as the digital image miraculously appeared on the wall-size screen behind the head of the table. Scratch that. Tessa King was a helluva lot more than attractive. Grayson averted his eyes from the picture of him staring into her beautiful face right before he'd placed his sunglasses on her.

So maybe it *did* look a bit worse than it was.

"Come on, you guys. The second she got into the main house and away from the cameras, she didn't even know I was there." Grayson heard the words come out of his mouth and prayed he didn't sound as though he was disappointed in being ignored. As a shift agent, he was supposed to blend into the background. He obviously didn't *want* to draw her attention. Or anyone else's for that matter.

"So you think she played it up for the cameras?" SAIC Simon studied him.

"No." Grayson sighed, wishing he could claim

that the whole thing was nothing more than an opportunistic stunt on her part. It would certainly stop all the eyebrows currently wagging in his direction. "The panic attack was legit. Just ask the medic who took her vitals afterward. I'm simply saying that the second she knew she was out of the woods, she didn't need my support anymore. Like I said last night, I only did what any other agent in my place would've done in the same situation. And I'm sure Miss King would've reacted the same way if Franks or Lopez, or hell, even Doherty, had been the one to catch her."

Simon shrugged. "Well, it doesn't matter who caught her. It matters that the media think they sniffed out a big story and they're not gonna let go when their teeth are locked into something this juicy."

Tessa was a news personality and probably on a first-name basis with most of the press corps. Couldn't she call them off herself? Grayson fought the urge to rub his temples. Not wanting to give the woman another thought, he asked, "What do we care if the sharks eat one of their own?"

"Because those sharks are currently surrounding the Twin Kings Ranch. Along with God knows who else trying to get a front-page-worthy pic. It's like the Wild West of paparazzi and reporters outside those gates right now. Nobody needs me to remind them of how John Hinckley Junior was able to get so close to Reagan in 1981, do they?" The room went quiet as everyone thought about how the would-be assassin easily blended in with members of the press right before he'd opened fire on the president. Simon cleared his throat before continuing. "Therefore, Agent Wyatt, as long as there is an ongoing threat to the King family, even if it's only from news cameras, you and half the team are staying here."

Grayson swallowed back several curses as he sat stiffly and listened to the protective intel agents outline the focus of their reconfigured assignment, conveniently titled Operation Snowball.

When everyone stood to leave the room, Simon motioned for Grayson to meet him near the now empty coffee machine. After making sure they were alone, Simon opened his laptop.

"Just a head's up, Wyatt. One of the local uniformed deputies in the staging tent yesterday was wearing their body camera and unknowingly recorded footage of Tessa King dressing you down and questioning your tactical decisions. The sheriff is going to do everything in his power to make sure the video doesn't get leaked to the press, but he already has his hands full, and it's only a matter of time before I have the chain of command breathing down our necks about the possibility of calling you before an inquiry board."

Grayson sighed. "Sir, I know that the hearse was an unconventional choice as far as extraction vehicles, but I stand by my decision to use the closest resource available while simultaneously keeping the primary location secure."

"I'm already writing that in my situation report. In fact, I'm keeping you in place on the ranch because I know I can trust you."

His boss made the decision sound like a reward, while the truth was that staying on assignment was a lose-lose situation. Even if Grayson wanted to tuck tail and run, which he never had before, it wouldn't do him any favors. He exhaled in defeat. "And because removing me from an assignment at this juncture might in some way imply that I was being punished or couldn't be trusted."

"That, too. You're a good agent and, from everything I've seen, you handled yourself with the utmost professionalism under the circumstances."

That may be so, given his supervisor's outside viewpoint. But deep down Grayson knew that he'd allowed Tessa to get too close to him. And while he hadn't acted in a way that technically crossed any professional line, there was no doubt his physical response to the woman had called that line into question. Sensing Simon wanted to say more, Grayson prompted, "But?"

"But..." Simon sighed. "My concern is that Miss King might not see it the same way."

The suggested threat of betrayal settled between Grayson's shoulder blades, as though he was already anticipating the knife to be shoved into his back. He'd saved Tessa from collapsing on those church steps for the entire world to see. Then he'd stayed by her side, intervening before she had another panic attack while literally holding her upright as she paid her last respects to her father. He'd even given her his favorite pair of sunglasses. "You think she'll file a formal complaint about me?"

"You think she won't?" Simon hitched a brow.

Grayson sucked in a deep breath, wishing he'd never been stationed on those church steps yesterday. That he'd never met Tessa King. "The only thing I think is that I really don't know her at all."

"Look…" Simon spoke as he packed his laptop into a waterproof case. "We all liked working with her father, and because of that, I want to give her the benefit of the doubt. But I've been in this business a long time. She's probably going to be embarrassed when she sees herself portrayed in an unflattering light. She's also going to have an entire public relations team working to turn this story around so she doesn't look bad. Hopefully, she can save herself without drowning you—or the agency—in the process. It's been my experience, though, that powerful people will do anything to protect their reputations, including throwing little minnows like us to the sharks in order to save themselves."

Grayson watched his supervisor leave before turning his attention back to the whiteboard at the front of the room. Unfortunately, he couldn't afford to sit here and worry about the outcome of a potential inquiry board or a media feeding frenzy. He couldn't even afford to think about how Tessa was going to react when she saw the videos or whether she would save herself. He had a job to do and the job always came first.

He could only pray that Miss King had a good PR person to get them both out of this mess. Because staying holed up on this ranch, no matter how many thousands of acres it covered, with the beautiful woman was going to be more dangerous than diving straight into shark-infested waters.

Chapter Four

"**W**hy do they always do this?" Tessa shoved her smartphone across the breakfast table so it would be far out of her reach. She needed to resist the temptation to scroll through any more pictures of her being carried away from her father's funeral by #SecretAgentSteamy, which was currently the top trending hashtag on every social media platform in the United States. And half of Europe.

"Because news sells," Aunt Freckles replied, taking a hot pan of her famous buttermilk biscuits out of the oven. "And sensational news sells sensationally. I would've thought they'd taught you that in Journalism 101."

"This isn't journalism." Tessa folded her arms in front of her in an effort to still her twitching fingers. "It's pure voyeurism."

"Can you blame the public, darlin'? That Agent Wyatt looks just as yummy as my freshly whipped honey butter." Freckles set down a ceramic crock full of creamy heaven in front of Tessa. "Get your knife ready because there ain't nothing my home-made biscuits can't solve."

"How did you sneak real butter past Mom?" Tessa peeked down the hallway connecting the kitchen to the rest of the house. Sherilee King's strict vegan diet was more about her waistline and less about her fondness for animals.

"I waited until after the guests left and your mom snuck off to that spot by the river where she and your dad used to go. She needs some alone time. Then I slipped MJ a hundred-dollar bill and the keys to your uncle Rider's truck yesterday afternoon to run into town and get me some."

"Couldn't you have just asked the catering staff to leave those little rectangle packets wrapped in foil?"

"Nope. Your momma gave the caterers strict orders to take every last pat with them when they left. Not that it mattered because I wouldn't dream of messing up my new polish unwrapping those darn things when the butter inside isn't even my brand."

Tessa glanced down at her aunt's long acrylic nails, which were now a different—and brighter, if that were possible—shade than they'd been at yesterday's funeral.

"Besides," Freckles continued, "your baby brother was champing at the bit to get out of here yesterday. I merely provided him with the means and justification to escape."

Tessa's mother must've heard that last part as she walked into the kitchen through the mudroom. "So you're the one to blame for Mitchell Junior getting arrested last night?"

"Arrested?" Tessa dropped her knife back into the ceramic crock. "For what?"

"For being out late with Kendra Broman." Sherilee picked up the warm biscuit already coated with butter from Tessa's plate, smeared on another two layers, then shoved half the thing into her mouth. Crumbs fell from her lips as she mumbled, "Two scandals with two of my kids in less than two days. It's like my heart isn't already breaking enough with Roper gone."

Freckles buttered another biscuit and handed it to her former sister-in-law. "Since when is it a crime for a young buck to spend a little time in the evening with a pretty girl?"

"Did I mention there was some underage drinking involved and Mitchell allegedly took a swing at the arresting deputy? Who also happened to be Kendra's *father*?"

"Did you call Marcus?" Tessa reached across the

table for her recently abandoned phone, intending to call her brother.

"Call him? I've been in his office for the past thirty minutes reading him the riot act. When that didn't work, I reminded Marcus that I suffered through twenty-six agonizing hours of labor giving birth to him. I swear, that boy refuses to listen to reason." Her mom lovingly gazed down at the biscuit that had magically appeared in her hand and sighed. "God, I'd kill for some bacon right now."

Freckles, who had an uncanny knack for knowing what people needed before they even knew it themselves, already had the seldom-used cast-iron skillet going. She caught Tessa's attention before nodding toward Sherilee and mouthing the words, *Stress eating.*

"So then where's MJ now?" Tessa asked her mom.

"Still in jail. Marcus is charging him with resisting arrest. I guess, technically, Deputy Broman is charging him with that. But Marcus is the sheriff and *he* thinks Mitchell needs to stay put until the arraignment this afternoon. *He* thinks his baby brother has been bailed out by his family too many times already and needs to learn a lesson. Apparently, *he* doesn't know that reporters are crawling all over town right now trying to get more dirt on *your*—" her mom pointed the butter knife in Tessa's direction "—little display yesterday."

Tessa inwardly rolled her eyes before throwing out

a half-hearted wave dismissing the accusation. Sure, she could defend herself. Again. Or calmly try to explain to her mother that the so-called "little display yesterday," was exactly that—little. She knew from experience, though, that arguing with Sherilee King was tantamount to waving a red flag in the face of an angry bull, and the woman would not be satisfied until she drew blood.

"I'm serious, Contessa." Their mom only used her children's formal names when she wanted to add that extra bit of drama. "We barely laid your father to rest and already he'd be rolling over in his grave with his children's scandalous behavior."

"Stop getting so worked up, Sher." Freckles flipped over a slice of bacon. "Roper King never let a little bit of scandal get to him. This'll all die down by tonight."

"It'd better." Sherilee jutted her chin toward the jungle-print yoga pants doing nothing to camouflage Freckles's curvaceous backside. "Because if I have to eat my way through any more stress, my rear end is going to end up as big as yours."

Freckles opened her mouth to fire back a response at her sister-in-law and Tessa knew she had to stop the two women before the name-calling made the situation worse. "Did you mention the reporters to Marcus?"

"Yes. His solution was to call the special agent

in charge and request additional agents stay on to secure the ranch."

Alarm bells went off in Tessa's head. She formed her lips to ask a question but the words got caught in her throat. Closing her eyes, she touched her tongue to the roof of her mouth, just like her former speech therapist had taught her. She concentrated and tried again. "Wh…wh…which additional agents?"

"Hopefully, not the one you got into trouble with yesterday," her mother replied, apparently not noticing Tessa's stutter.

"Sorry to disappoint you, Sherilee." Freckles wiggled her heavily penciled eyebrows as though she weren't the least bit sorry. Or disappointed. "But it doesn't look like Agent Steamy is packing his bags anytime soon."

The legs of her mother's chair screeched against the wood-planked floor as she scrambled to look out the large picture window that framed the kitchen table. "How can you tell?"

Tessa, hoping to be less conspicuous, remained firmly planted in her seat. Yet she couldn't help stretching her neck to see around both her mom and her aunt.

An all-terrain vehicle with two men in suits pulled onto the dirt road behind the house, followed by another all-terrain vehicle that parked behind them. The second ATV was driven by a woman dressed in dusty boots, jeans and a flannel shirt. Her leather-tooled belt holding a black-leather holster was the only giveaway that she wasn't actually working with the cattle today.

Climbing out of the seat beside her was a man dressed as though he'd just bought his outfit at the Wild West costume shop yesterday. That turquoise snap-button paisley shirt still had the fold creases in the material, which seemed to strain across his broad shoulders. And he was wearing hiking boots instead of actual cowboy boots. Okay, so maybe his well-worn jeans didn't look so brand-new. In fact, they molded to his muscular thighs like they were made for the man.

Tessa gulped and forced her eyes above his narrow black belt, which didn't boast any sort of ornate rodeo-style buckle most of the other ranch employees wore. Agent Grayson Wyatt had to be the worst undercover cowboy she had ever seen.

Unfortunately, the shiver of awareness racing down her spine reminded her that Grayson looked just as attractive as he had yesterday.

Tessa used one of the monogrammed linen napkins to wipe away the dampness that suddenly appeared above her upper lip. She'd thought she'd put yesterday's panic attack out of her mind last night. But then she'd awoken to both the internet and her mother all abuzz this morning. Now, the cause of the incident himself was walking up to the back porch wearing his brand-new shirt, causing her nerve endings to tingle with the threat of disaster.

Even though she knew it was coming, the loud knock on the kitchen door reverberated in her throat.

"Come on in." Freckles's welcoming grin was as wide as the pit growing in Tessa's stomach.

"Is now a good time for that family briefing?" the special agent in charge asked the three women in the room.

"Well, half of our family isn't even here, Agent Simon. But you already know that since you were down at the sheriff's office earlier." Sherilee's tone was accusatory, as though it was somehow the Secret Service's fault that MJ had gotten arrested.

"Mom," Tessa warned before turning her attention to the SAIC, carefully avoiding looking past him to Grayson. "I'm not sure we need a formal briefing. Dahlia lives in town and Duke and his husband are on the same flight to DC with me this afternoon. It'll just be my mother and my sister Finn staying on at the ranch. Oh, and MJ. When Marcus releases him, of course."

"Oh no." Her mother pointed a butter-smeared finger at Tessa. "You are not flying to DC this afternoon and leaving this bodyguard mess behind for me to clean up."

"What mess is there to clean up?" Finn King asked as she brushed past the four agents huddled near the doorway and planted herself in the center of the kitchen. Finn had probably been wide-awake and out roping calves well before dawn. That was why she was the heir apparent to the Twin Kings Ranch. She was the only sibling fully devoted to working the land. "The steers hate those ATVs, by the way. I'd appreciate it if your agents wouldn't race them pass the chutes on the mornings we're trying to breed."

Tessa had never been as happy for her little sister's take-charge attitude as she was right then. Nothing happened on the ranch without Finn knowing about it. And if Finn didn't want the agents sticking around, they'd be out of there by midday.

Sherilee rubbed the one crease in her otherwise cosmetically enhanced forehead before turning to her youngest daughter. "Maybe if you weren't so busy playing matchmaker with your precious bulls, Finn, you'd know that other *humans* in your family are still going through the grieving process."

"Mom, those bulls pay for all this." Finn extended her arm to gesture from the entire house and its professionally decorated contents to the rolling hills outside. "Besides, us *humans* all grieve in our own way. My way is to continue the Twin Kings' dynasty. Apparently, MJ's is to get stupid drunk with Deputy Broman's daughter. And Tessa's way is to make headlines with Agent Steamy over there."

A warm flush spread through Tessa's face and she refused to address the Agent Steamy comment while the man in question was only a few yards away, his calculated gaze seemingly absorbing every detail in their kitchen. Instead, she smiled at her sister and asked, "Does part of the Twin Kings' dynasty involve stomping through the house like a herd of wild elephants with your muddy boots?"

Normally, their mother would've taken the bait and immediately scolded anyone who dared to track so much as a speck of dirt into her pristine home. But she was too focused on pouring the entire contents of the china cream pitcher into her coffee.

"Nice try, Tess." Finn grabbed a biscuit off the plate and shot Aunt Freckles a wink. "But the only elephant in this room is the one between you and Agent Steamy and the hundred cameras stationed along every fence line hoping to get another picture of you two in a compromising position."

Yep, Finn was very well aware of what was going on at the ranch and she had no problem speaking her mind. She'd inherited their father's love of the land, but not his skills at diplomacy or his ability to keep family matters private. Tessa gave her little sister a warning glance and Finn responded by sticking out her lips and making kissing noises.

"With all due respect, Miss King and Miss King," SAIC Simon interjected. "When the media gets wind of your younger brother's arrest, you're going to have paparazzi rushing the gates trying to get the inside scoop. Several of them have already extended their reservations at the hotel in town because of the, uh—" the supervisor briefly glanced at Tessa "—'Agent Steamy' incident. So even if that situation dies down, like it usually does, we're not comfortable abandoning our post just yet."

Grayson cleared his throat. "Can we please stop referring to me as Agent Steamy?"

"Nope," Aunt Freckles said.

"Not a chance," Finn echoed.

"You two are absolutely incorrigible," Sherilee scolded as she stood from the table, pretending not to see all the flaky biscuit crumbs falling from her tailored silk blouse to the floor. "Agents, I apologize for my *youngest* daughter and my *former* sister-in-law. They both know better than to ogle random men and tease employees of our government."

"Mom, aren't you gonna apologize for your *oldest* daughter, as well?" Finn asked not so innocently. "Pretty sure Tessa knows better than to fall into the arms of strange men, no matter how swoon-worthy they are."

"I didn't fall." Tessa shot Finn a look that promised retribution. "He picked me up."

"Technically, you were on your way down." Grayson's mouth quirked up on one side as he corrected her. And to think she'd actually had a dream last night about that mouth of his—

Tessa snapped to attention, squelching the thought as soon as it began.

"What was that all about anyway, Tessa?" her mother asked. "Usually, you have no problem in front of the cameras. Was it the shoes? I know you're friends with that designer, but the heels were way too high and pointy for those narrow steps."

"It wasn't the shoes, Mom." Tessa assumed her mother had been too overwhelmed by everything and everyone yesterday that she hadn't noticed the not-so-discreet exit from the church. If Sherilee had caught wind of what had actually happened, it would've become an even bigger circus with medical specialists called in. Her mom had enough to worry about as it was. Tessa casually flicked her wrist. "We can talk about it later."

"Was it your foundation garments?" her mother continued, refusing to drop the subject. "You might want to switch to Spanx. They're less likely to cut off your circulation."

"Good lord, Sherilee," Freckles said. "Tessa wasn't even wearing a girdle yesterday."

"I didn't say *girdle*," Sherilee whispered the last word. "That would've been beyond tacky to discuss in front of company."

Tessa, her face flaming and her head pounding, shot Finn a pleading look. *Say something!*

"Oh, come on, Mom." Finn might get a kick out of teasing her siblings, but when it came to anyone else doing the same, she was always the first to jump in and defend them. "Couldn't you tell that Tessa had another one of her panic attacks yesterday?"

"No!" Sherilee gasped and Tessa suddenly wished Finn hadn't been so quick to stick up for her. "When did they come back? I thought you'd gotten beyond all that."

"I was beyond it, Mom. I mean I *am* beyond it. That's all in my pa...pa... In my past."

Sherilee shot to her daughter's side and pressed the back of her hand to Tessa's forehead, as though checking for a fever. "All this stress is too much for you. Your neurologist said this could happen, but it's been so long and you've worked so hard. You should stay on at the ranch. I'll fly the speech therapist out. More press is going to mean more scrutiny. If your stutter comes back, you're not going to want to be in front of a camera."

"Mom!" Tessa raised her voice to drown out her mother's ongoing concerns then gave a pointed look toward the four agents, who had been discreet up until this point. Though, when all of this was over, who knew what any of them would say in their tell-all memoirs?

"Don't shout, Tessa. It'll only make you more frustrated and then you won't be able to get the words out at all." Her mom's heavy diamond ring, the one she hadn't dared remove in over thirty years, threatened to tangle in Tessa's hair. Her mother's anxiety tended to escalate a situation rather than defuse it.

It was a stark reminder that Sherilee was the worrier of the family and Roper had been the soother. Tessa winced when the thick gold band inadvertently thunked against her throbbing temple.

"Oh no. Your headaches are coming back, too."

"They are now," Tessa muttered.

"Leave her be, Sher." Freckles stepped up beside Sherilee and put an arm around her waist, leading the distraught woman away from the kitchen before anything else was said in front of Grayson and the other agents.

But the damage was already done. The words her mother had spoken aloud only echoed the unspoken fears Tessa had fought to squelch last night. Could the recent trauma of losing her father possibly cause a relapse? Could all of those symptoms she'd once overcome after her TBI be coming back to haunt her? While her forehead pulsed with crowded thoughts, the space under Tessa's rib cage felt hollow and she resisted the urge to wrap her arms around herself. God forbid the ever-astute Agent Grayson think Tessa was weak or needed some sort of emotional support. Again.

But Tessa was already exposed. And her mom was right. She should probably consult with a neurologist or someone and get her stress under control before she returned to DC. Before she returned to the lights and cameras in the studio and made another mess of herself on live television.

* * *

Grayson wasn't any clearer during the official family briefing in the conference room than he'd been inside the Kings' kitchen earlier that morning. He knew powerful people liked to keep their secrets, but this family was on a whole other level. So what if the world found out that Tessa King had panic attacks or stuttered once in a while?

And Mitchell Junior wasn't the first eighteen-year-old to get into a little trouble with the law. He certainly wouldn't be the last.

"It seems like it would be a lot less trouble to just give the press their story, then let them lose interest," Grayson suggested to the family members sitting around the briefing room table. "They always do."

"Darlin', this must be your first assignment with the King family." Freckles patted his shoulder sympathetically, as though he was inexperienced or too naïve to understand. "They don't like to admit defeat. It's not in their blood. Hell, Rider still hasn't signed our divorce papers and we've been separated for over fifteen years now."

"It's true," Rider said, pushing out his barrel chest. "Grandma Millie and my Marine Corps drill instructors most definitely did *not* train me to surrender. You were Special Forces like me, Wyatt. You know we fight to the last breath."

Tessa's eyebrows lifted at the mention of Grayson's prior military career, which he hadn't shared with the other civilians in this room. Apparently, though, this family had their own recon team working for them. They probably knew just as much about him as he did about them. For the hundredth time today, Grayson clenched his jaw while wishing he had joined the DEA. Or the FDA. Or any other agency that didn't have to deal with the Kings and their inability to stay on task.

"Let's not talk about last breaths, under the circumstances." Mrs. King sniffed, returning to her role as grieving widow now that there were an additional fifteen members of the protective division team in the room with them.

Grayson had to admit, he'd enjoyed the verbal sparring between the King matriarch and her two daughters earlier in the kitchen. Some of his team members had referred to Sherilee King as a diamond-studded battle-ax. Clearly, they hadn't met the younger King females. Anyone who went against the combined forces of Finn and Tessa King had to be sharp and strong enough to withstand the verbal blows.

His father, a former football coach, had always said iron sharpens iron. *"To be the best, you have to practice against the best."* When it came to verbal assaults, the Kings sure as hell kept each other sharp.

That brought Grayson back to his original train of thought. "My point was that if you hold a press conference and answer their questions, they'll hopefully lose interest and everyone can move on. The

King name is certainly strong enough to withstand the fallout from the scandals."

"First of all…" Tessa finally spoke up. "We already have a public relations team working on how to spin this. Second of all, it's not a scandal. At least the one involving me and you isn't a scandal. Yet. But if they find out that you're still on the property and they think we're in close contact, that's only going to fuel their speculation."

"I agree," Grayson was quick to reply. After all, he didn't want the woman—or anyone—thinking that he hoped to stick around any longer than he had to. "Unfortunately, as SAIC Simon already pointed out, removing me from the assignment would be tantamount to admitting that I—that *we*—did something wrong. Or had something to hide. And clearly that's not the case."

It was important to reiterate that he'd followed procedure and hadn't done anything wrong. He'd overheard the earlier conversation about Tessa's history of panic attacks and her stuttering. It was the second time he'd witnessed the way she'd tried to steer certain conversations away from herself. Obviously, there was something more she wanted to hide. Grayson just didn't want her using him as a shield, hiding whatever secret she had behind him. Or behind his career.

"I'm with Agent Wyatt," Duke King said, leaning back in his leather chair. The second child of the

King family was assigned the code name "Peace-keeper," and after watching Tessa's brother calmly interacting with every member of the family during yesterday's gathering, the name was well-earned. "If *you* make this into a big deal, everyone else will make it a big deal."

"I seem to remember Dad saying the same when you wanted to have a small wedding a few years back. But even he couldn't stop the paparazzi from trying to crash his perfect son's reception."

"Perfect is *your* word, not mine." Duke shrugged. From what Grayson had read about the man in the briefing file, he was a high school football legend, graduated top of his class from Annapolis before flying F/A-18s for the Navy. Hard to beat that kind of resume. Finn pretended to flick a piece of mud off her boot and onto his crisply starched uniform. He glanced at his younger sister. "Knock it off, Runt."

"Make me," Finn said then actually sent a clump of dried dirt flying toward the target of Duke's creased pants.

Duke's husband, Tom, whose similar service khakis had the Medical Corps insignia on the left collar, laughed. "Direct hit."

"Real mature, you two," Duke countered as though he were too important to stoop to their teasing. When Finn turned her head, though, Duke got his revenge by flipping the brim of her Dorsey's Tractor Supply ball cap upward and causing the sweat-stained hat to fall on the ground. Apparently, even a peacemaker had his limits before he'd seek retribution. Not that Grayson could blame Duke for putting an annoying little sister in her place.

Grayson had used to play fight with Maddie the same way before she'd gotten sick. Wait, this was play fighting, right? Grayson asked himself when Finn used the fallen cap to smack her brother's biceps. Duke dodged just in time, though, and Finn's blow landed on Tom instead.

Marcus King let himself into the room and Grayson hoped the sheriff was prepared to get between his squabbling siblings. Or at least steer this sinking ship back on course. Then he heard Sherilee King snort and Grayson braced himself for yet another rogue wave to knock them off course.

"So glad you could take a break from your busy schedule of locking up innocent children and join us," Mrs. King said.

"Mom, MJ is eighteen," Marcus sighed. "He's not a child anymore, and he certainly isn't innocent."

"That's not what his lawyer says." Mrs. King crossed her arms over her chest.

Marcus's eyes narrowed. "You didn't actually hire *her* as his attorney, did you, Mom?"

There were several loud intakes of breath around the conference table and even Duke and Finn paused from their play wrestling to pay attention.

Was there another family scandal in the works?

Stay in your lane, Grayson, he told his throbbing head. Mitchell Junior wasn't part of his assignment. Echo Team could deal with this during the second part of the briefing. He looked at his watch.

Agent Lopez apparently didn't share Grayson's desire to get out of the conference room anytime today and asked, "Who is 'her'?"

"Marcus's ex-girlfriend," Freckles said in a stage whisper that everyone in the room heard. "She was in town for the funeral. Her mother is—"

"Hey, Aunt Freckles," Tessa interrupted. "I'm sure the agents are getting very bored with all our family's drama. They need to get back to…whatever it is they need to do."

Yep. This family had plenty of secrets. And Grayson truly didn't want to be a part of any of it. He cleared his throat, resisting the urge to tell Tessa that "whatever it is they need to do" involved protecting her from overeager photographers and anyone else who might sneak onto their property to get a juicy story. Or do something worse.

Grayson tapped a key on his laptop and brought up the next slide on the overhead screen. "So let's go over the perimeter weaknesses and the procedures for entering and exiting the property at the check-in stations."

Finn groaned and Tessa sank lower into her seat as Grayson spoke.

He tried to keep from looking in Tessa's direction

as he discussed the terrain and the fence lines and potential entry points, but it was difficult to *not* see her out of the corner of his eye. Difficult to *not* think about how she'd felt in his arms yesterday.

When Grayson finished his presentation, he moved to the back of the room and chugged an entire bottle of water. Mentally, he felt as though he'd just hiked fifty clicks through the mountains of Afghanistan. Actually, he'd done exactly that during one of his military deployments and it had been a heck of a lot easier back then. And filled with considerably fewer land mines.

As long as he could shield Tessa from any more unexpected media coverage, though, the whole Agent Steamy story would die down and his mission would be a success. That by itself wouldn't be a challenge. The problem: the only way Grayson could protect her was by staying close to her.

Chapter Five

As Lopez went over her list of Twin Kings Ranch employees and authorized guests, Grayson finally allowed his eyes to roam Tessa's profile.

She was even better looking without all that makeup on, but her mouth was tenser than it had been yesterday. Her blond hair was pulled into a loose ponytail and she was wearing a soft gray sweater and a pair of black pants, which looked both expensive and tight in all the right places.

When he'd seen her in the kitchen earlier, she'd been wearing a loose pair of men's-style pajamas. He'd been thinking about what had been underneath that plaid flannel for the past three hours. Just like he was currently wondering what she was hiding underneath that cool façade of hers. Sure, she was maintaining her perfect composure now, but yesterday he'd seen her go from completely vulnerable to a profanity-laced tirade and back to vulnerable.

It was that tirade, though, that kept Grayson from hopping on the first jet out of Wyoming. He was a professional and he'd done his job. If the video of her yelling at him in the staging tent was leaked, there was a chance he would find himself in front of a disciplinary board. And Grayson didn't do disciplinary boards.

Hell, he'd never so much as gotten a tardy slip in elementary school. And that was saying something considering his dad's job at the local high school started early and his mom was usually busy with his sister and wasn't always available to get him to class. He'd had to learn at a young age to manage his own needs and make as little work for his parents as possible. Then after his dad passed away, he'd not only had to take care of himself, he'd had to help his mom with his sister.

Speaking of Maddie, he wanted to call her back before he went on duty tonight. He checked his watch again.

After another ten minutes with Marcus and Sherilee King exchanging pointed glares at each other across the table—and Duke and Finn physically poking at one another under the table—Lopez finally asked the question Grayson had been waiting for. "So who else will be staying on the ranch?"

"Me!" Finn raised her hand. "In fact, I rarely leave."

"And it shows," Duke added. "You could use a little more socialization."

"Children," Mrs. King said to the two grown adults scowling at each other playfully. At least, Grayson hoped they were being playful. There was no telling with this bunch.

Duke straightened his already straight tie. "Tom has three surgeries scheduled for tomorrow at Walter Reed. Originally, we were going to leave for the airport after the briefing, but now I'm thinking someone should stay and be the voice of reason in this family. Plus, my commander called me unexpectedly this morning and gave me leave for the rest of the week."

"He better have," Mrs. King mumbled, then cleared her throat. "I mean, what a nice surprise. I don't think I could get through this without you, Duke."

"Kiss up," Finn accused, but Grayson noted the younger woman now had her arm linked tightly through her brother's instead of shoving him away. Almost as though she wasn't ready for him to leave either.

Lopez, like a teacher trying to get her rowdy class's attention, tapped the two names she'd written on the whiteboard. "Anyone else?"

"I'll be staying on the ranch, obviously," Mrs. King said. She made eye contact with Marcus and added, "So will Mitchell Junior, once the judge releases him."

"I live closer to town," Marcus told Lopez, wisely ignoring his mother's prediction. "But my twins usually come back here after school when I'm working. I pick the boys up around six in the evening and we sometimes stay for dinner. Unless my mom decides we're not welcome anymore."

"Don't be ridiculous, Marcus. I'd never turn away my own family. Unlike some of my children, one of whom I went through twenty-six agonizing hours of labor with to only have them stab me—"

"What about Dahlia King?" Lopez interrupted, looking down at her binder. "Will she be here at all?"

"Dia," Finn corrected. Grayson remembered the info packet he'd received on the King family. Finn and Dahlia were twins, with Dahlia being older by three whole minutes and regarded as somewhat of the family's black sheep. Or lone wolf, depending on who one asked. "She lives above Big Millie's Saloon in town. Her daughter, Amelia, also comes here after school and for riding lessons, so she'll be in and out."

Sherilee sighed at the mention of the saloon and Grayson realized Dahlia's chosen profession was another bone of contention within the King ranks.

But there was one family member who hadn't responded to Lopez yet.

"And you?" Grayson asked, looking at Tessa. "Did you decide if you're staying or going back to DC?"

"I—I'll maybe stay for another day. As long as Duke is here to run interference for me."

Grayson glanced at Duke in time to see him hold up two fingers as if he was pledging the Boy Scout oath.

"Put her down for at least a week," Sherilee told Lopez.

"I'm not staying for a whole week, Mom." Tessa rubbed at the cute little crevice above her nose. "I have a job."

"Your father died, Contessa. I'm sure your audience will understand if you don't hop right back on the air. I'll speak to your producer—"

"No, Mom. He threatened to change his number after the last time you called him. Besides, it's not just my job. I also have a life."

"Then have Congressman Townsend come visit here. Put him on the list," her mother told Lopez.

"No," Tessa said again. "Don't put him on the list."

"Did you break up?" Rider and Freckles asked in unison. The elderly couple had definitely perked up at the possibility.

"No. Not exactly." Tessa's eyes flicked toward Grayson, but when he refused to look away, she focused on a spot past Grayson's head. "We can talk about this later."

So there *was* trouble in paradise. His gut had been right. At least he still had his instincts going for him, even if his sanity was slowly slipping.

"Keep him on the list," Sherilee King repeated to Lopez before turning to Tessa. "It'll look better for the PR team if he visits and your relationship seems solid."

Lopez shrugged. "We can always take him off if things don't work out."

"Think of it as a hotel reservation," Duke suggested. "Except no charge for a cancellation fee."

"Do you think he's going to dump you after this?" Finn asked, clearly ignoring her sister's request to talk about the subject privately. Or maybe in spite of it.

"Never," Marcus replied for Tessa. "Congressman Smooth loves the limelight and the family connection too much."

"Speaking of family connection..." Mrs. King shot another sharp look at Marcus before returning her eagle eyes to Tessa. "I'd appreciate having as many of my children here in Wyoming for as long as possible. After all, the next time they'll all be under the same roof will probably be at my own funeral."

Grayson shifted in his chair. If *his* mother had laid on a guilt trip like that, there was no way he'd be able to refuse her wishes. But Noreen Wyatt would never go that route. His mother was the most selfless woman he knew, and didn't have a strategic bone in her body.

And right now, Grayson needed to go call her to get away from the constant headache the King family had given him.

"So tell me about the food at this new treatment facility," Grayson said to his younger sister whose face occupied the screen of the laptop. She was twenty-eight years old, but looked more like a teenager in that big hospital bed. "Is it any good?"

"Can we *not* talk about my upcoming procedure for a few minutes?" Maddie replied. "I want to talk about my big brother's picture being posted all over the internet like some sort of prince charming rescuing a damsel in distress."

"Don't let Tessa King hear you call her a damsel, let alone one in distress."

"Tell me about her."

He resisted the urge to make sure none of the other agents in the bunkhouse could hear him. They could sniff out suspicion from a mile away. "Even if I were at liberty to disclose that information, there's nothing to tell, really. I hardly even know her."

"Oh come on, Gray. I'm going stir crazy over here practically waiting to die."

"Maddie, you're not going to—"

"Don't say it. We always promised not to lie to each other." His sister's body might have atrophied over the years, but her silver eyes were as fierce and determined as ever. He'd never seen them lose their light, no matter how grim her prognosis had been. "This treatment doesn't have a guaranteed success rate on someone my age. And even then, I'm only holding off the inevitable a few more years."

"If you would let me finish..." he continued, refusing to even acknowledge any possibility that the spine fusion wouldn't work. "I was saying that you're not going to go stir crazy with that new laptop. Which, by the way, I got you so that you can work on that online masters program. Not so you could run internet searches on me. If you're bored, you need to be studying."

"How can I keep my mind on anything right now? Please, Gray. Give me something to live for."

The familiar guilt twisted inside his chest.

Growing up, he'd been the big brother who'd done all the physical stuff his sister hadn't been able to do. Maddie had been diagnosed with Emery-Dreifuss Muscular Dystrophy, or EDMD for short, when she was nine years old. There'd been no stopping the weakening of the muscles in her shoulders, upper arms, calves and legs. There'd only been physical therapy and sometimes surgical intervention to relieve the stiff joints of her elbows, neck and heels. Surgical release of the contracted muscles sometimes helped, but never kept the contractures from recurring.

They'd known that conduction blocks would eventually start affecting Maddie's heart, disrupting the heartbeat rhythm since the electrical impulses wouldn't communicate between the upper and lower chambers. She'd gotten her first pacemaker two years ago. Now she was having rods inserted into her spine to hopefully keep her walking so she could maximize her physical therapy.

Nothing was wrong with her mind or her sassy attitude, though, Grayson thought before asking, "Where's Mom?"

"I made her go get a coffee down in the cafeteria. You think I'd be using that 'something to live for' line if she was in the room with me? I'm not that heartless."

"Sorry. I've been with the cruise director of guilt trips lately," he said, thinking of Sherilee King. "So I'm a little suspect of everyone right now."

"Right now? Gray, you're always suspect of everyone. It's what makes you so good at your job." His sister's eyes twinkled. "Now tell me about your next assignment. Are you going back to the White House?"

"First of all, you know I can't divulge that kind of information. Second of all, I'm still on my current assignment for an undisclosed amount of time."

"So you're staying on that fancy ranch in Wyoming?" Maddie asked but didn't give him time to respond. "Can you send me pics of the inside of the house? I saw an article about the Kings in *Fine Tastes* and there were all these glossy pictures of a huge mansion made to look like a rustic log cabin. The kitchen was bigger than our entire apartment."

Grayson didn't want to admit that the kitchen was in fact twice as big, if one counted something called a butler's pantry and the separate prep area for catering staff whenever the Kings had a party. "Since when do you read snooty magazines like *Fine Tastes*?"

"Since my big brother insisted on paying out of pocket for only the top-rated specialists. All those plush waiting rooms have magazines like that."

Their mom, who had always been Maddie's sole caretaker, hadn't been able to work full-time after their dad died, so their government-subsidized medical insurance only covered the basics. Grayson would've put them on his own insurance plan if he could. Instead, he worked as much overtime as possible so that his sister could have the best health care possible. And so that his mom could afford to take hotel rooms near the hospitals and pay for meal deliveries when she was too tired to cook after spending the day driving Maddie around to doctor and physical therapy appointments.

Neither Noreen nor Maddie would ever ask him for so much as a dime, but if he couldn't be home to take care of them himself, the least he could do was send a part of his paycheck to help.

His dad had always hoped Grayson would get

a football scholarship right after high school, but he hadn't wanted to waste time on college when he could join the Marines and immediately start earning a paycheck to send home.

"Did the screen freeze?" Maddie asked.

"Huh?" Grayson replied.

"You were just sitting there not answering. I thought the video connection had gone out again."

"Sorry, I was just lost in thought."

"About the beautiful and smart Tessa King?" His sister wiggled her pale eyebrows.

"What? No. I mean other than how she relates to my afternoon shift. Speaking of which, I've got to go back to work. Tell Mom to text me when you get out of surgery."

Maddie shrugged. "Give me Tessa King's number and I'll have Mom text *her* instead."

"The painkillers must already be taking effect if you're crazy enough to think I'd ever give you top-secret information like that."

Maddie's eyes narrowed playfully. "So you *do* have her number."

Actually, he didn't have Tessa's number, though he could get it from the Protective Intelligence Division. "Don't need it. And I definitely don't want it."

"You need *some*one, Grayson. Mom is worried that you haven't dated anyone since Jamie."

Grayson shook his head, trying to dislodge the sting of the reminder. "I *need* to get back to work.

Good luck in the operating room and try not to yell at the nurses this time."

"I didn't yell at that nurse. I politely told her that I didn't appreciate them putting me in a hospital gown covered with pink and purple unicorns. I don't care if they thought it fit me better. I'm a twenty-eight-year-old woman. Not some preteen with stars in her eyes."

"Says the grown adult who is addicted to sour gummy bears." He smiled indulgently. "Love you, Mads."

"Love you more, Gray."

He closed the screen of his laptop, disconnecting the video call. He hadn't lied to his sister. He really did need to get back to work, which meant he had to get his mind right. If Grayson couldn't do his job, then he couldn't provide for his sister, which was the indirect goal of all of his missions. All the hours of training, the overtime shifts, the high-risk assignments came at a physical cost for him, but the financial reward was well worth with it. But that also meant compartmentalizing his family life and his work life, and even his social life—not that he had much of one. He couldn't allow himself to be distracted by thoughts of his sister's medical procedure, or by what the internet was saying about him.

Or the fact that Tessa King had just ridden by the bunkhouse on a horse, without an assigned agent trailing at a distance.

Crap. He'd been in the briefing with her and knew

she'd heard the part about having an agent accompany her everywhere she went. He'd also seen her roll her pretty blue eyes at that particular directive. That meant she must've purposely slipped her tail. Doherty was supposed to be assigned to her this afternoon. Grayson should simply let his fellow team member deal with the woman.

Unfortunately, his job was to protect *all* the Kings. Even the ones who'd been assigned to someone else.

Even the ones who made his muscles tense and his blood heat up.

"I know I told you I'd be back on the air by tomorrow night, Bryson," Tessa told the chief executive of programming at her network. Her agent had offered to make the necessary calls for her, but Tessa hadn't become one of the top political analysts on prime time TV by avoiding the tough conversations. "But a few things have come up and I need to stay in Wyoming another week."

"I told you that you should've planned to take the full week," Bryson Johnson told her before speaking to someone else on his end of the line—probably his assistant. "Get Brett Monroe from the morning roundtable show and see if he can cover the eight o'clock slot this week."

"You know, Brett Monroe didn't do well in focus groups when he covered the gubernatorial debates last summer," Tessa reminded her boss. After all, this was *her* show they were talking about. Her name was in the title. *Bottom Line with Tessa King.* No way was some comedian-turned-breakfast-show host going to maintain the serious integrity of the very program Tessa had built. "I'd go with Juanita Munoz. She covered that election scandal in South America and—"

"Fine," Bryson interrupted. "We'll send Brett up to Wyoming for an exclusive on you and that Agent Steamy guy."

"No, I'm not going to comment on the Secret Service agent who was doing his job. We both know that's nothing but tabloid fodder and our network is better than that."

"Hmm. You might be right. Probably not a good look to be talking about your love life on camera so soon after your father's passing. Plus, if you're hiding out, that'll build up the speculation. As long as you don't hide out so long that everyone forgets about you."

"It's only a week, Bryson," she tried to reassure him, though they both knew that in this business, there was always another big story and a hungry journalist right around the corner. "Besides, it's also not a good look for the network to be spinning my family's tragedy to their advantage."

"Damn, Tessa. I'm sorry. You're right." He paused. "Did you get the flowers we sent?"

"The flowers were beautiful," she replied carefully. There'd been so many arrangements delivered to the church and the ranch, she'd had no idea who had sent what. But all flowers were beautiful, weren't they? And she appreciated the gesture, even though she knew that Bryson was probably more concerned with the potential loss of viewers than with Tessa's personal loss. "So I'll see you in a week."

"Of course. Take all the time you need. We'll schedule your exclusive with Brett for March sweeps instead."

Tessa knew better than to tell her boss that there was no way she was going to do any sort of interview about her love life, especially with someone like Brett Monroe. However, that was a battle to be fought after she secured her next contract. At the end of the day, she couldn't blame her network for wanting to capitalize on her personal situation. It was a business, and they were there to make money. Unfortunately for them, there was no story to sell.

When Tessa got off the phone with Bryson, she sent her agent a text with the contact info for her mother's public relations team. After all, those weren't the tough calls, just the annoying ones.

She could hear Aunt Freckles banging around in the kitchen and, as much as she loved the older woman, Tessa didn't want to be within a mile radius when Sherilee found out her former sister-in-law was making chicken-fried steak and gravy for dinner.

Tessa sat back in the stuffed leather chair in front of her father's desk. She'd come into his office to make her call, but she hadn't dared to actually sit *be-hind* his desk. This room was her father's sanctuary and there were parts of him everywhere she looked. Pictures of him with celebrities, world leaders and military buddies shared space with family photos and homemade Father's Day gifts.

She picked up a frame with a black-and-white photograph of Roper and Rider when they were only seven years old. The towheaded boys were dressed in matching denim overalls and had their arms over each other's shoulders. Their identical noses were covered in freckles and their wide grins were missing at least six teeth between the two of them.

Tessa's heart tugged at the obvious closeness of the little boys. Even though they'd grown up to live such different lives, there were no two men who had loved her more. She shuddered as a sob threatened to make its way through her chest.

If she were smart, she'd let herself have a good cry and get it over with. But once she started, there'd be no stopping the flood of tears that was sure to come. And who knew who might walk in and see her?

She needed to get outside, to get away from all the memories inside the house. When Tessa had wanted to get away from the stresses of childhood, she'd go to the swimming pool her parents kept heated eight months out of the year and practice her dives. But after her accident, her mom had removed the diving board and Tessa had a feeling that seeing the empty spot where the board used to be would be worse than sitting in her father's study.

In DC, she'd work out to relieve some of the antsiness, but she was pretty sure her mom was with a personal yoga instructor in the home gym right now. And Tessa really didn't feel like being around anyone.

She stood and stretched. The entire backside of the house was covered in floor-to-ceiling windows that framed the glorious purple mountains in the distance. Maybe she should go for a ride. She hadn't been on a horse for a few years and relearning the motions would require her to think about what she was doing, which would be way better than going for a mindless jog where her brain might latch onto any passing thought.

She found a pair of extra boots in Finn's closet and, because they weren't the type of sisters who shared everything, Tessa decided it was better to borrow now and ask for forgiveness later.

One of the stable workers offered to saddle a mare for her, but Tessa declined, needing physical activity that required her to get outside of her own head.

She and Phoebe—Finn had named the mare when she'd been going through her *Friends* phase—started off on a measured pace.

Tessa got the older horse up to a slow canter but, rocking back and forth in the leather saddle, she decided it was *not* like riding a bike. She didn't remember her thighs ever burning this much before. Or needing to stretch her lower back. And she'd only gone a couple of miles or so. This might not have been her best idea.

She turned her head to gauge the distance and caught sight of someone riding up the path behind her. Tessa initially felt relief that she was no longer on the trail alone. Then she realized the person appeared to be even more awkward than she was on the back of a horse.

None of the hired cattle hands wore shirts that bright or sunglasses that dark. An electric current shot through Tessa's legs as Grayson Wyatt drew closer.

"Sorry to intrude, Miss King, but we discussed this in the briefing this morning."

"Discussed what?" she asked, wishing she'd brought her own sunglasses again. Instead, she pulled the brim of her dad's old University of Wyoming cap lower.

"Members of the family shouldn't go anywhere without an escort."

She looked at the Teton mountain range in the distance to make sure she hadn't gone farther than she thought. "But I'm not leaving the ranch."

"Still." That was all he said and she swallowed a groan of frustration.

Not that she needed an explanation. Tessa wasn't about to play stupid with him and pretend like she didn't know full well that someone could slip through one of the checkpoints and gain access to them. It was a vast, sprawling property, not Fort Knox.

She was about to turn around and head back to the stables—her sore forearms gripping the reins certainly would've appreciated that. But she saw how uncomfortable the perfect agent was on his own horse and decided she could suffer his presence a little longer if it meant putting him outside *his* comfort zone for a change.

Tessa snapped the reins and urged Phoebe into another canter, the thrill of regaining control overriding her protesting muscles.

Chapter Six

Grayson could go for hours and hours without talking to a soul. It was one of the skills he'd mastered as a sniper for both the Marines and the Counter Assault Team.

Following Tessa King, he didn't say a word—not even a warning when she rode under a sagging tree branch and almost didn't duck in time. Occasionally, he'd hear another agent on his earpiece, yet for the most part, it was blessedly uneventful and quiet everywhere else on the ranch. By the time she passed the trail that would take them back to the stables, though, she was slouching so low that he wasn't sure how much longer she could remain upright in the saddle.

"Do you know where we're going?" he finally asked.

"Of course I do." She slowed her pace until his horse was beside hers. "At least, I used to. But it'll come back to me."

Grayson didn't need the GPS on his watch to tell him exactly where they were. On the airplane here, he'd studied the trail maps while other agents had studied nearby restaurants that served the best steaks and coldest beers. Plus, the horses had already done at least two circles right past this location today. "There's a creek about half a mile from here. We should probably stop and get the horses some water."

She exhaled and gave a stiff nod. "As much as I hate to admit it, you're probably right."

Instead of pulling ahead of him on her horse so that he could once again follow behind her at a respectable distance, she allowed her horse to remain abreast of his.

"You hate admitting when someone else is right?" Grayson asked then immediately wished he'd kept his mouth shut.

Their roles were already defined and there was no room for crossover. He was the agent and she was the assignment. It wasn't that he felt he was inferior to her in any way—except maybe financially. Nor did he care about the fact they came from two different social worlds. His job, though, depended on them staying in their roles. Walking along side by side once again made them equals and blurred those boundaries between them.

The military had a rule about fraternization between officers and enlisted personnel and, in Grayson's mind, this situation was no different. It would certainly be easier for him to do his job if he didn't have to think of Tessa King as anything other than an assignment.

"I don't mind someone else being right." She exhaled and he tried not to stare at the smooth skin along her neck. "I just hate being wrong."

His mouth twitched. "Are you ever wrong?"

"Only when I told myself that riding this horse would be like riding a bike and that I'd remember what to do as soon as I climbed on. Unfortunately, my thighs and lower back have completely forgotten all the muscle work involved."

Grayson allowed his eyes to trail down her legs encased in snug denim. "Your muscles seem to be doing just fine."

He heard the breath hitch in her throat over the sound of the water flowing through the nearby creek. Grounding his back molars in place, he reminded himself of those damn boundaries. *She's a job, not a woman.*

The problem was he knew how to talk to a woman. He didn't know how to make polite conversation with a job.

"I mean, you haven't fallen yet. Not that you normally fall…" He trailed off when she lifted one eyebrow at him.

"You know, I really don't go collapsing in front of strangers. Yesterday was a one-off," she said then proceeded to dismount with more grace than she probably felt.

Don't look at her rear end, he warned himself as he climbed out of the saddle. But as he used the reins to lead his horse to the creek, his eyes went straight to the curve of her backside.

He cleared his throat and scanned the area for any sort of threat, whether it be a wild animal or a bold trespasser wielding a weapon or, worse, a camera. He radioed in their location and got an update from the command center.

They stood along the bank as their horses drank greedily from the stream. He rubbed his hand along the gray gelding's back and murmured a few words of appreciation to the poor animal who'd had to carry his awkward two-hundred-pound frame this far.

"Chandler likes you." Tessa finally broke the silence.

"Who?"

"Chandler Bing. From the TV show. Finn wanted to move to NYC and share an apartment with all her best friends before she decided to become a cowgirl instead. She named these two—" Tessa gestured toward both horses "—along with several others.

That's why their row in the stables is referred to as Central Perk."

Grayson chuckled, the vibration in his throat feeling unnatural. "My sister is a big *Friends* fan, too."

Maybe when this assignment was officially over and debriefed, he'd be able to share that detail with Maddie. She'd appreciate a stable full of horses being named after characters in her TV series.

"Well, I hope your sister rides better than you." Tessa smirked.

"She used to. Hopefully, she will again."

"Is she okay?" Tessa asked as her cheeks turned a charming shade of pink. "Sorry. Asking personal questions is a habit from work."

Grayson could count on one hand the number of agents and military buddies who knew about his sister's condition. Maddie had hated all the pitying looks and curious stares she'd gotten when their mother or Grayson would have to push her custom-made wheelchair on her bad days. So his way of protecting her was to pretend that there was nothing wrong in front of outsiders.

Yet the concern on Tessa's face was sincere and, after all, Grayson had brought up the subject of his sister.

"She has a rare type of muscular dystrophy. When we were younger, our family went to this camp where kids with special needs got to ride therapy horses.

The place was called Let's Ride and that was their motto. The first time they put her up on that great big horse, I immediately demanded that they get her off. She's always been tiny and her muscles are easily weakened. I didn't think she could handle such a huge animal. But she took to it like that—" Grayson snapped his fingers. "Maddie was doing the jump course by the end of the week."

"And what about you? Did you do the jump course?"

"No way. The only reason I got on the horse was so that I could trail behind her and pull her to safety if something happened."

"Of course. A born rescuer. Did anything ever happen?"

"Not that week." His pointed look conveyed his belief that nothing was going to happen this week, either. At least, not on his watch.

"So did Maddie get her own horse when you guys got home from camp?"

"We lived in a duplex in a subdivision outside of Baltimore at the time. So even if we could've afforded one, there wouldn't have been anywhere to keep it. Or ride it."

"Where does Maddie live now?" Tessa asked. "Maybe there's a nearby equestrian program where she could take riding lessons or at least visit the horses?"

"I found a horse farm an hour away from their apartment in Baltimore. It's supposed to be for children with special needs, but they made an exception for Maddie because she looks like she's twelve years old. She'd be so pissed if she knew that because she hates being mistaken for a kid. Anyway, she used to ride whenever she was wasn't suffering from contractures." And when Grayson could send some extra money home to pay for the lessons. "She's having surgery this afternoon to get a steel rod implanted along her spine. It's not a guaranteed procedure, but if it works, she'll regain some of her mobility and might be able to ride again."

Tessa studied him for several moments and he waited for the questions that were sure to follow. But all she said was, "Your face softens when you talk about your sister. Actually, it softens when you talk, period."

Grayson's only response was to scan the horizon and keep his mouth clamped shut. It'd been easier to do his job when they weren't talking and she wasn't noticing how soft or not his face was.

When the horses finished drinking their fill, Tessa led Phoebe up the bank and toward an old wooden post that might've been part of a fence at one point. Apparently they weren't heading back to the stables anytime soon.

She must've read his mind because she offered,

"I just need to stretch out a few more minutes before I get back in the saddle."

She looped the reins around the post and then did some yoga-style poses. Man, this woman was flexible. She lifted her arms over her head before slowly bending to touch the grass below her boots.

Grayson's throat tightened and he averted his gaze, staring at the icy cold water rippling over the rocks as it flowed down the creek. Was it deep enough for him to fully submerge his head? It was either that or be tempted by the view of her thighs as she lunged deeply, her hips dipping low.

He heard Agent Lopez speak into the radio at the same time he heard the familiar whirl of helicopter blades. Grayson's adrenaline kicked in and he hooked his arm around Tessa's waist and yanked her against his side, immediately rushing her toward the closest oak tree, where the thicker branches provided them better cover.

Tessa wrapped her arm around Grayson's waist as she huddled behind him. He had a feeling it was instinctive, but it threw him right back into his role of protector.

He remained planted in front of her as he walked both of them backward so that she was positioned between him and the thick tree trunk. Placing two of his fingers on his earpiece, he copied the radio exchange then relayed the information to Tessa.

"There's an unidentified helicopter circling the property. No station logo or anything else to identify it from their vantage point. It's currently staying above a thousand feet and isn't showing any sign of landing. Do you know if anyone in your family is expecting a visitor?"

Tessa poked her head around his shoulder. "Not that I know of."

Chandler snorted at something in the sky and then stomped his front foot. The sound of the helicopter grew louder and the horse took off for parts unknown.

Damn.

Of course Grayson's first instinct had been to get Tessa to safety before securing the horse. He was a special agent, not a cowboy. Thankfully, Tessa had tied Phoebe to that post. But the mare tugged against her reins, whinnying as though she was about to run off with her stable mate.

"Stay here," he commanded Tessa before approaching Phoebe with both arms outstretched in what he hoped was a calmness that defied his current adrenaline level. When he reached the loose knot in the reins, the mare used her nose to shake her head away from him. He'd prefer to bring the horse under the tree, but he didn't want to risk her fighting him and taking off after Chandler.

"It's okay, girl," Tessa said, coming around his

shoulder, blatantly ignoring his instructions to stay put. "I'll hold her bridle. You retie her."

The helicopter passed overhead just as he got the reins secured tighter. They sprinted toward the overhanging branches together, but not before he spotted a logo on the green paint. Buster Chop's Chopper Rentals.

Grayson spoke into his mouthpiece, advising the team of the logo and the tail number identifying the aircraft's registration. "A large oak tree is currently providing us with suitable visual coverage for now, and I don't believe our position has been compromised yet."

"Copy that," Lopez replied in his ear. "Be advised local air traffic control hasn't authorized any aircraft to be in our no-fly zone and the unsub is not responding to attempts at radio contact. Intercepting authorities are en route and should be on scene in two clicks."

"I've got a visual of the unsub from the eastern trailhead," Doherty added. "Appears to be a telephoto lens aimed out the open hatch of the aircraft. Maintain your current position."

"10-4," Grayson said and exhaled, somewhat relieved that it wasn't something more deadly aimed out the open hatch. Tessa lifted questioning eyes to his face and he told her, "They think it's a photographer. But it keeps circling the area above us, so something must be giving our position away."

"It's probably a scared horse running around with an empty saddle." Tessa pointed to a field in the distance where Chandler was anxiously galloping in circles. "Poor guy was probably heading back to the stables, but the helicopter followed him and now he's just racing in a loop. I need to go get him."

"Negative." Grayson moved in front of her again and reached behind both their backs to press her against him before she could inch forward. The helicopter dipped lower, making the leaves above their heads rustle each time it dropped down. "We need to stay in position. If the horse is scared, he won't come to you anyway."

"I can't just hide under here," Tessa protested.

Grayson wanted to argue with her, but he knew the exact feeling. He hated hiding when he could be doing something way more proactive to protect her.

The sound of an approaching aircraft—make that two approaching aircrafts—drowned out all other arguments.

"Are those fighter jets?" Tessa peeked around his back to scan the horizon. "So much for pretending like my being at Twin Kings is no big deal."

Even though he knew she was only echoing his own words from the earlier briefing, they still had to follow standard protocol any time their team was actively deployed. "Several military jets are on standby at the nearby airfield. A couple of them were dispatched to remind Buster Chops up there that this is a no-fly zone."

The helicopter must've taken the hint because after several seconds, the roaring engines and blades above trailed off until they no longer could be heard.

Grayson's hand was still on the back of Tessa's waist. He loosened his grip, but she didn't immediately pull away.

"The helicopter is bugging out," he said into the radio before running his palm along her lower spine in what he hoped was a soothing motion. Unfortunately, the feel of her breasts still pressed against his back didn't soothe him. He cleared his throat and then took a couple of steps before shifting to face her. "We should be getting the all-clear any minute and then we can return to the stables."

She turned her eyes up to his and, instead of seeing fear or even annoyance reflected at him, they held a tinge of amusement.

"What's so funny?" he asked.

"Unfortunately, there are two of us and now we only have one horse."

Tessa took pity on Grayson and walked alongside her mare instead of hopping back in the saddle and making a mad dash for the stables. After all, she should have waited for one of the agents to accompany her on the ride in the first place.

Not that she'd needed anyone's protection from

the big bad cameraman hanging out of the helicopter. She did just fine dodging paparazzi back in DC, mostly by pretending that they didn't even exist. However, the Secret Service agency had a job to do—no matter how much Tessa resented their intrusion or Grayson Wyatt's high-handedness.

By disrupting their protocol and leaving without her protective detail, she could've caused a lot more work and worry for the team tasked to locate her after realizing she was gone. These men and women were putting their lives in danger to protect her and her family, and taking off like that without a thought of the added workload they'd face was selfish on her part.

Although, to be fair, she hadn't really gone very far.

"Did you know that we'd been riding in circles when you followed me earlier?" she asked the man walking beside her.

Grayson gave a stiff nod, his boots steadily keeping her slower pace even though she had a feeling he could run to the stables and back before she made it another mile. He didn't seem nearly as exhausted as she felt. In fact, with his shoulders squared off and his head on a swivel, he looked as though he was on a mission and wasn't going to rest until he'd accomplished his goal.

"Why didn't you say anything, then?"

"Wasn't my place," he said, causing a wave of

shame to wash through Tessa. Just because she hadn't wanted him there didn't mean she thought of him as the hired help—someone under her authority who should be seen and not heard.

What happened to that guy a couple of hours ago who'd been talking about his sister and her specialized riding program? Grayson had almost seemed like a real person such a short time ago. But then the helicopter showed up and he'd gone right back into special agent mode. Devoid of expression or even emotion.

Not that a simple conversation earlier meant they were suddenly best friends or anything. Just like the heated looks he'd given her in the briefing room this morning didn't mean that he was attracted to her. An unexpected warmth rose along the back of her neck at the memory and she resisted the urge to lift her hair and fan herself.

Instead, Tessa pulled an insulated bottle from her saddlebag and took a long drink, hoping the cool water would lessen some of the heat coursing through her on this unusually sunny January day.

Normally, she was in command of a situation. In fact, two years ago she'd won the Walter Cronkite Award for Excellence in Television Political Journalism because she hadn't backed down during her interview with one of the most powerful dictators in the world.

It was like playing a game of chess. Getting the

other person talking about themselves was key to them letting down their guard. Once their defenses were lowered, Tessa could usually steer them in the direction she needed them to go.

Not that she needed to steer Grayson into some sort of news-breaking headline. But if she could get him talking—or otherwise acting like a normal human being and not a robotic bodyguard—Tessa wouldn't feel as though she required his protection. Or anyone's protection, for that matter. Even if she couldn't take charge of the situation, the least she could do was put them on some sort of level playing field.

"Do you know that most fish and birds use sun compass orientation to migrate to the same breeding ground years later?" She offered him her bottle of water.

"Was that what you were you looking for today, Miss King? A particular breeding ground?" Grayson asked as he took the bottle. Tessa immediately averted her eyes so that she wouldn't see his lips on the exact same spot where her mouth had been seconds ago. Unfortunately, her eyes landed on his neck and she was so transfixed on watching his throat muscles move that she tripped on a rock.

"My point is that I used to know these trails like the back of my hand. But now, everything about this place seems so different."

"Well, you've been under a lot of stress with your

father's passing and your, uh, family…" He took a deep breath before wisely letting that sentence trail off.

"Drama?" she offered.

"I was going to say 'dynamics.'" He smiled and Tessa's knees grew so wobbly she would've for sure gone down if there'd been another rock in her path. If the press had captured Grayson Wyatt's sly grin, the pictures from the day of the funeral would have been captioned a lot more graphically than "Agent Steamy."

Remembering the press and the reason he was there, Tessa sucked in a quick breath to shore up courage. "Listen, I'm sorry for taking off without an escort earlier. It's been a long time since I've had a protective tail, but I still know the rules."

"Luckily, nobody was in any danger. This time." His warning hung in the air between them.

"Anyway, I just needed to get out of the house and clear my head. I hadn't meant to be gone so long. But, like I said, everything out here looks so much different since I moved away. You could've spoken up sooner if you'd known I was lost."

"And risk being called…oh, what was it you said in the staging center tent yesterday? An 'overbearing, overcompensating a-hole with a hero complex'?"

Tessa flinched. Last night, Marcus warned her that one of the local law enforcement officers in the staging area yesterday had been wearing a body camera on his ballistics vest and inadvertently recorded the whole thing. She still hadn't seen the footage and, unfortunately, with everything else going on yesterday, she couldn't recall the exact words she'd used. "Look, I'm sorry if anything I said offended you."

"I wasn't offended," he replied, his smile long gone. She watched his jaw tighten before he continued. "I was doing my job, by any means necessary."

"I never wanted to be part of your job, though," Tessa said, pushing her shoulders back. She needed him to see that she could protect herself. Of course, how could she convince him of that after she'd been so quick to run and hide behind his broad, muscular back as soon as the helicopter showed up? *Don't think about his back!* Tessa straightened her spine. "I never asked for any of this."

He didn't respond for a few moments and Tessa figured he was back in his silent protector mode. Then he cleared his throat. "Your family made a few comments this morning about you having a history of panic attacks and something about a stutter—"

"Oh no!" Her hand shot to her mouth before she could stop it. "I didn't stutter in that video yesterday, did I?"

He tilted his head to one side, as though trying to figure out how to answer her question while still drawing more information from her. It was a tactic she'd used herself when she interviewed guests on her show.

Tessa tried a different strategy. "You know what? Forget I asked that. Let's talk about something else."

"Like the weather?" Grayson looked up toward the cloudless sky. "It's fifty-eight degrees and sunny. Very unusual for Wyoming this time of year. What do you want to talk about next?"

I want to talk about you*!* Tessa wanted to yell. *Tell me everything about Special Agent Grayson Wyatt.* Of course, she was better trained than to lead with such an open-ended and personal question. Instead she asked, "How about you tell me where you got that ugly shirt?"

He chuckled, but walked several more steps before finally answering. "I borrowed it from Agent Doherty, the guy with the Red Sox hat who was running the projector this morning during the briefing."

"But you're so much bigger than…" She paused when he turned his head toward her, as though he was suddenly very interested in having *this* particular conversation. A tingling sensation raced through her.

"Not that I was checking out your body or anything," she quickly said then felt the heat return to her neck. "I mean, it just seemed like the shirt was a little small on you. Not that it matters. Some people like tight clothes."

Lord, she needed to shut up.

Grayson's eyes traveled down the jeans she'd found in Finn's closet, the ones that Tessa had to wrestle over her hips a few hours ago. Everything suddenly felt tighter, including her own skin, as she waited for him to answer.

She was one second away from grabbing the saddle blanket and wrapping it around herself like a shield when he finally responded. "My boss wanted us to try to blend in with the other ranch employees and I only packed suits and workout gear because I thought it'd be a short trip."

She suddenly had a vision of the man in running shorts and a sweaty T-shirt, his massive chest rising and falling with each exerted breath—

"I had to borrow everything I'm wearing, too," she blurted out in an effort to shut off the fantasy playing through her mind. "Except my underwear, of course. Oh geez! Please forget I said that. My powers of speech never fail me when I actually need them to."

"I will definitely add that to my list of things I need to forget about you," Grayson said, however, his slow, appraising stare suggested he was doing the exact opposite. That he was, in fact, committing every detail about her to memory.

Unable to withstand the heat from his gaze, she began walking again, ignoring the trickle of sweat between her shoulder blades. She bit her lower lip to keep from saying anything else as they approached the stables. Next time Tessa went for a ride, she would ask the female agent to accompany her. Agent

Lopez at least dressed as though she knew her way around a ranch and horses.

But if she made that request, would everyone think that something had happened between her and Grayson today? That could make the situation worse.

Ugh, Tessa screamed inside her head. Why was she suddenly overthinking every little thing?

Maybe she shouldn't go riding again at all, she thought as she unsaddled Phoebe inside the stables. Duke might be willing to go with her, but he flew jets for a living and thought horses moved too slowly. Which meant that if he went with her, then she'd have to play that stupid fighter pilot video game he'd found in the den. Her brother might be the peacemaker of the family, but only because he was a brilliant negotiator. And as much as Tessa loved spending time with Duke, she wasn't about to pick up a game controller and get virtually shot down by someone who'd been trained on actual jets.

Maybe instead of riding, she could just use the home gym, or go for a long run to stretch out the muscles she'd overused today.

But the following morning, after a heated argument between Marcus and Marcus's ex-girlfriend—who had agreed to be MJ's attorney for his drunk and disorderly charge—Tessa found herself heading straight for the stables again to get away from the drama.

This time, though, she didn't have to wait for an agent to come find her. Grayson was already inside waiting for her.

Chapter Seven

Just like the day before, Grayson followed Tessa at a respectable distance after they set out on Phoebe and Ross, a gelding with a black coat and a spiky mane. Chandler had thankfully returned to the stables on his own yesterday—just in time for the evening feeding—and snorted his annoyance at Grayson before grudgingly taking an apple as a peace offering. The stable foreman assured him the older stallion would be fine after his adventure, but should probably rest another day or two before going on any more rides.

They were only half a mile onto the trail when Finn and Duke raced by on another pair of horses, causing

Grayson's and Tessa's mounts to draw closer together. He could practically feel the gears in Tessa's mind shifting, as though she was contemplating breaking their mutual silence. As soon as her lips opened, Grayson beat her to the punch. "So, uh, how long has your family owned this ranch?"

Of course Grayson already knew everything there was to know about Twin Kings. It was in his preop briefing notes. But maybe if he could get her talking about something other than his sister or his job or why he was still there, then he wouldn't slip into talking about himself. Like he had yesterday.

Tessa took the bait and nudged her mount along. "The King family first settled in Wyoming in the late 1890s. But it wasn't on this ranch. My dad used to tell the story about his great-grandmother, who was on a train heading to Oregon to teach at a school in a mining town there. But her train was delayed in Teton Ridge because US Marshals were looking for several members of the Black Hills Bandits who were reported to be stowaways trying to leave the state."

Grayson might've grown up a city boy in Baltimore, but he was a sucker for a Wild West adventure story. "Never heard of them."

"They were a gang of robbers out of Deadwood, South Dakota. Trains, stagecoaches, banks—these guys weren't picky. Anyway, she fell in love with the town and, after the marshals interviewed everyone on board and sent the train on its way, she

stuck around. The story my dad *didn't* tell the public
was that his great-grandfather was actually one of
the Black Hills Bandits and Big Millie—that would
be my great-great-grandmother—had discovered
the youngest and most charming member of the
gang hiding in her travel compartment on board the
train. She'd felt so sorry for the handsome bandit,
she didn't alert the conductor. In fact, when it was
her turn to be interviewed, she told the marshals that
she and the young man had been travelling together
since Laramie, which wasn't a total lie. So, she fell
in love with the town as well as a notorious criminal
who promised that he could change his ways with
the love of a good woman."

"And did he change his ways?" Grayson asked.

"Only for the first year. He left her with a baby to
raise by herself before he skipped town. Since only
single women without children could be schoolteach-
ers back then, Big Millie turned to any means necessary to support her daughter."

"So that explains how Big Millie's Saloon in town
got its start," he said before taking a swig from his
water bottle.

"Actually, it got its start as a brothel."

Grayson choked on the water.

"Aha, I bet you didn't read about *that* little tid-
bit in your top-secret King Family file." When she
smiled, she had a dimple on her left cheek that somehow made her look softer, less standoffish.

Easy, Wyatt. Dimple or not, Tessa King was still an assignment.

He wiped his mouth with the back of his hand. "I definitely would've remembered those kinds of details. So your great-great-grandfather was a train robber and your great-great-grandmother was a madam. Was King even their last name?"

"Who knows? People reinvent themselves all the time. Luckily, this all happened way before the worldwide web made public records so accessible."

Grayson didn't want to think of the other things—or pictures—that could easily be found on the internet. "So I'm guessing your great-great-grandmother eventually decided to go straight and bought the ranch?"

"Nope. Although, when Prohibition started, she was making so much money selling bootleg, she closed down the upstairs rooms. Little Millie, her daughter, took over the daily operation of what was then the most popular speakeasy in Wyoming. See, Little Millie had fallen in love and gotten pregnant by a local boy who'd died in France during World War One. But since she and the local boy hadn't married before he'd gone overseas, his family refused to accept my grandfather as their heir."

"Hmm," Grayson murmured. He knew he should offer a more sympathetic comment, but he'd save that emotion for after he met with the family's PR team and was convinced the rest of the Kings weren't in the habit of denying responsibility for their actions.

"Anyway, Little Millie, wanting her only son to have more than a brothel-turned-saloon as his legacy, won a thirty-acre cattle ranch in a poker game and put it in Hank's name. When Hank's wife gave birth to a pair of boys, they renamed the ranch Twin Kings."

Grayson pointedly looked around at the wide expanse of meadow and mountains around them. "This is a lot bigger than thirty acres."

"Fifty-five thousand, eight hundred and twenty-two at last count," Tessa confirmed. Grayson didn't own so much as a houseplant, so he couldn't relate. "Over the years, Hank bought out the neighboring ranches and when his sons came home from Vietnam, they steadily acquired more acres and built the ranch to what it was today. My dad was the businessman and the networker, while Uncle Rider was the foreman and the cattle expert."

Grayson nodded. "Okay, this part I know. Rider stayed in the original cabin on the other side of the stables and bunkhouses while Roper built a house fit for royalty."

"Technically, it was my mom who insisted on the house built for royalty. She really likes to play up the last name King." Tessa rolled her eyes.

"Is that why your first name is actually Contessa?" Grayson didn't mention that he'd learned that bit of trivia in the briefing file after overhearing her mother call her that in the family kitchen.

"Hardly seems fair that you know so much about me and my family yet I know so little about your background." Tessa slowed her horse when they approached the same stream where they'd stopped yesterday. "Speaking of which, how did your sister's surgery go?"

Grayson swallowed his surprise. Tessa had been so animated talking about her family's history, he hadn't expected her to shift gears so suddenly. And he especially hadn't expected her to remember anything about *his* family. Really, they shouldn't be talking about families at all. Or anything else, for that matter. But as she dismounted, her blue eyes were full of curiosity and remained fixed on his face. He couldn't dismiss her question without seeming like a heartless jerk.

"It sounds like the procedure went as expected. She's on a lot of pain meds and the recovery is going to be pretty rough. They won't know how successful it was until she's able to start her physical therapy."

This was the part where Tessa would nod politely and start doing those yoga stretches again, her question forgotten as soon as she'd asked it. Instead, she tilted her head to the side, her loose ponytail brushing her shoulder. "I read that sometimes the spine will refuse to completely fuse to the rod. Do the doctors have a backup plan in place in case that happens?"

"You read up on my sister's procedure?" It was difficult to hide the surprise in his voice. So he joined her on the ground before leading his own horse to the water.

"Well, I have a tendency to read up on everything. My dad used to call me his research archaeologist because I like to dig for information." Tessa shrugged, causing a strand of blond hair to come loose and frame her face. "I've always been interested in neurological conditions, though. And, last night, it was either listen to my mom and Freckles argue about the trans fat levels in chicken-fried steak, or go to my room and do some research."

"Oh," was all Grayson could manage to respond, keeping Ross's reins firmly in his hand as the horse drank from the creek. He didn't need another runaway horse on his record.

"Sorry, I didn't mean to suggest that your sister needed a backup plan. Obviously, you should stay positive and I'm sure that everything will be fine."

"No, we're being realistic about our expectations. It's just that…" Grayson paused, trying to think of the most delicate way to put this without disclosing his family's limited finances. "Well, we're taking her condition one day at a time. It's difficult to plan ahead since a lot of the procedures that could ease her conjectures are experimental and not covered by insurance."

"Of course," Tessa said, finally looking away. In his experience, people didn't like to be reminded about uncomfortable things like diseases and disparities in wealth. Just when he'd thought he'd found the way to keep her from asking anything else about his family, she asked, "Has your mom been with Maddie since yesterday?"

His sister's name rolled off Tessa's lips so casually, Grayson had to resist the urge to pretend he was receiving an important communication in his radio earpiece. His toes twitched inside his hiking boots as he forced himself to stay put and not literally run away from the question.

"Would you rather not talk about this?" she asked, concern etched across her forehead. It was one of those pitying looks the hospital staff used to give him and his mom. One of those looks that suggested the Wyatt family wasn't strong enough to go through something so difficult.

His shoulders drew back. "No, I was just surprised that you remembered my sister's name."

"You know the names of all of my siblings."

"Yeah, but it's my job to know everything about you." Heat burned behind his ears and he had a feeling they matched her red woolen jacket. "I mean about your family. You guys are my assignment."

"Are we back to that again? I'm just a job to you?"

He exhaled deeply. "I'm trying to remain professional."

"Then treat me like another professional. Hell, treat me like your coworker. Just don't treat me like I'm some snot-nosed kid you're babysitting."

"Fair enough," he conceded. "We're just a couple of professionals with the same goal—to keep you out of the public eye."

"Thank you." She nodded, her chin seeming more stubborn than ever before. "Now, as your coworker, do you have anything going on in your personal life that might be a distraction from you effectively completing your duties?"

"I always complete my duties." His feet moved into a wider stance. "I don't get distracted."

Tessa lifted one perfect brow. "Even when your sister is in the hospital and you're worried about who might be there taking care of her?"

As much as he resented being on the other side of the interview chair, he respected her tenacity. She must be damn good at her job, because Grayson knew she wouldn't relent until she got an answer to her original question. "My mom is with Maddie in the hospital."

Technically, his mom hadn't been allowed to stay in the hospital overnight, so Grayson had booked her a room at a nearby hotel. But he had a feeling the bed hadn't even been slept in. As much as Noreen Wyatt needed the rest, she'd probably paced the floor all night, calling the nurses' desk every two hours for a status report.

Yet Grayson wasn't going to offer any additional information about his family. And to keep her from following up, he put his palm over his earpiece and said, "Excuse me while I radio the command center and give them a status report."

He walked his gelding back to the oak tree where he and Tessa had hid out yesterday from the helicopter. Grayson called in his location to the agent on communications duty, but, as expected, there was nothing new going on at the ranch. Despite her attempts to claim they were coworkers, the truth was that he was stuck out here on babysitting duty, his job talents being wasted on a woman who could clearly take care of herself.

He almost wished another helicopter would show up. Or that some desperate paparazzo would crash through the barricade at the gate. Anything that would provide some sort of action, something that would require him to prove himself as a trained law enforcement officer.

His muscles were coiled together much too tightly and he needed an outlet.

He could only work out at the gym so many times a day. Some of the other agents were going to go into town tonight after their shift, and Grayson decided he might tag along and give his adrenaline a little excitement. Not that he was one who got a kick out of going to small town bars and drinking with the locals, but it would be too dark to go rock climbing and Finn King had already chewed them out about racing their ATVs too close to the cattle pastures.

"You getting a little stir-crazy over here?" Tessa asked, practically reading his mind.

"What do you mean?"

"Your fingers are twitching and you keep rocking on the back of your heels. Plus, you're no longer pretending to be talking into your earpiece."

"I wasn't pretending…" He let the words trail off when she put her hands on her hips, her challenging stance only serving to draw his attention to her narrow waist. He gulped before forcing his eyes upward. "I keep expecting something to happen. But it's just so quiet out here. Not that I mind the quiet. Patience is normally one of my best qualities."

"Normally?" She quickly seized on the word. At this point, nothing about Tessa King's skills at observation should surprise him.

Being patient was one of the things that made him so good at his job, but admitting that would make him sound cocky. And he didn't need Tessa thinking he was both cocky *and* overprotective. Instead, he asked, "Are you planning to ride for much longer? The command center will want to know our ETA so they can brief the next agents coming on duty."

"We can head back now so you can finish your shift." She put her foot into the stirrup and easily swung up into the saddle. "At least *you* can leave the ranch."

She began to trot away and he had to heft himself into his own saddle, wincing at his sore backside before following after her. As his horse picked up speed, he realized they were almost at a gallop and he had to hold on for dear life. He clenched his jaw to keep his teeth from rattling around inside his head as he bounced at full speed down the trail.

He'd wanted an adrenaline rush, but the looming risk of falling off a horse and breaking his neck wasn't quite what he'd had in mind. Plus, Tessa's riding skills had suddenly returned and she was yards ahead of him, her rear end moving rhythmically as she leaned forward over her mare's neck.

So far they'd established that he wasn't a babysitter or a cowboy. So then where did that leave him when it came to doing his job? This damn assignment was more than testing his patience.

By the time he caught up with her, she'd slowed her horse to walk the rest of the way to the stables, and her chest was rising and falling more rhythmically than her butt had been a few seconds ago. One look at her parted lips and Grayson had to adjust the way he was sitting in the saddle.

Maybe it was sexual frustration or maybe it was how he'd seen his life flash before his eyes when the dirt trail had narrowed over by the canyon a few seconds ago. But before he could stop himself, he said, "You could leave the ranch, too, Tessa. You're not a prisoner."

In fact, his job would be way easier if she left. If she returned to DC.

Her hair had come completely loose and she shoved a handful of curls behind her ear. "That's the first time you've used my name."

He cleared his throat and sat straighter in the saddle. "Sorry about that—"

"Don't you dare call me Miss King," she interrupted, her eyes narrowed. "I think we're well beyond that."

Perhaps *she* was past that. But *he* needed to go back to the formality. He needed those boundaries. "I'll talk to SAIC Simon. I'm sure there's somewhere in town that we can secure in advance so that you can get out of here for a little while."

She waved off a young cowboy who'd eagerly run up to assist her out of the saddle. Tessa King didn't need a man to help her and she was making sure everyone knew it, including him. "Good idea. Tell him I'm going to Big Millie's."

Grayson watched as she led her horse away, her long legs taking purposeful strides, before he realized she wasn't joking.

Crap.

Thanks to his big mouth, now he was going to have to make sure she didn't get into trouble at some old brothel.

* * *

Why in the world had she wanted to go Big Millie's? Tessa asked herself for the fifth time that evening. Probably for the same reason her sister Dahlia had refused their mother's repeated pleas to change the name of the establishment. It made them feel more normal, more human, to have some connection to their family's not so illustrious past.

Okay, so maybe a small part of her had also been hoping to shake up the stiff and quiet Agent Wyatt by suggesting the bar outing. In fact, she'd have bet money that the guy would have declined this particular duty assignment for no other reason than to avoid her.

She'd have lost that bet.

Her sister normally didn't have many customers on a Tuesday night, so it wasn't like Dahlia was losing much business by closing early for Tessa and the ten Secret Service agents—five of whom were off duty—who'd accompanied them tonight. In fact, Dahlia was probably making more money since she'd doubled her prices and added a ten percent private party fee to each check.

Two agents were stationed outside the front door and two were stationed by the door in the alley. Finn and Duke had hopped into the black SUV with them at the last minute, and Marcus said he'd stop by with the twins after their basketball practice. Dahlia was behind the polished walnut bar, but the only people drinking anything stronger than beer were four of the off-duty agents.

Tessa wasn't clear on whether or not Grayson was technically working since she hadn't seen him take any time off. Not that she'd been watching him the past couple of days.

Tonight, like any other time, he refused to sit down, passed on a game of darts and didn't so much as tap a toe to the Garth Brooks's song playing on the jukebox. In fact, Grayson spent most of his time pacing back and forth between the front and rear doors to check in with the other agents. It was hard to ignore him when he kept in constant motion.

The man didn't know how to take a break.

Big Millie's part-time cook was off tonight, so Aunt Freckles, who owned the Cowgirl Up Café in Idaho and was also going stir-crazy at the full-staffed ranch, had offered up her skills as a short-order chef. Dahlia's five-year-old daughter, Amelia, came downstairs from their apartment and wanted to hang out with the adults.

"Have you learned how to make a Shirley Temple yet?" Finn asked their niece who handed Tessa a basket of onion rings.

"Mommy said it's a state law that I'm not allowed to touch the grown-up drinks or go behind the bar with her. So I'm helping Aunt Freckles in the kitchen 'cause I'm only allowed to be down here when we're giving away food."

"When we're *selling* food, Peanut," Dahlia corrected. "If we give all our food away, we won't ever make any money."

"Gan Gan says we have lots of money already, Mommy. She says you could buy me a whole zoo if you wanted to."

Tessa, who was sitting on the same side of the refinished wood bar as Finn and Duke, lifted her brows at their mother's latest attempt to sway one of her children into a different profession.

"But I don't want to work at a zoo," Dahlia said simply. "I want to work here. And when you grow up, you'll get to work wherever *you* want. And do you know why?"

"Because we're smart women who make our own choices, Mommy," the little girl replied with an adorable smile before lifting an empty plate over her head and carrying it back to the kitchen.

Tessa was always impressed with how great a mother Dahlia had turned out to be. She often wondered how she'd do as a parent if she had kids of her own. Or if she even wanted kids at all. Her eyes landed on Grayson across the room and suddenly her rib cage felt unnaturally tight.

"You really were the smartest one of all of us, Dahlia," Duke said before taking a long swig from his bottle of imported beer. "Owning your own business means you don't have Mom calling your boss—

or the Joint Chiefs of Staff in my case—to make them give you the week off with bereavement pay."

"Not until Mom gets the liquor laws changed in the state, which she's probably been trying to do. But until then, Amelia's right. Minors are allowed to be in the bar area as long as we serve food. No matter what some new guy who waltzes in off the street thinks."

"What new guy?" Duke asked.

"The cowboy who just inherited the Rocking D," Finn replied.

"How'd I miss this latest development?" Tessa wondered aloud.

"He's not a real cowboy," Dahlia said a bit too quickly. "And you probably missed it because it's been a weird week with other more important things going on. So what's going on with you and your Secret Service agent over there?"

"He's not *my* agent," Tessa said before biting into a crispy, golden onion ring. "Ouch!" She fanned a hand at her scalded taste buds before swallowing several gulps of frosty beer to ease her burning tongue.

"Careful." Finn scooped the basket of rings away from Tessa and offered one to Dahlia. "The onion rings are almost as hot as your agent."

Dahlia and Finn shared matching smirks. They'd been identical when they were girls, but sometime during high school, they'd gravitated toward separate identities and separate styles. In fact, most people were surprised to find out that the women were sisters, let alone twins.

They may be as different as night and day from each other, but when the twins shared a common goal, nobody else in the family would dare to go up against them. And right now, their goal was to keep Tessa from having any sort of break from the ongoing speculation about her and Grayson Wyatt.

"If I wanted to talk about my love life—" Tessa blew on a french fry before pointed it at Finn "—I'd have invited Mom to come along. Or the countless reporters camped outside the ranch gates."

"At least you *have* a love life." Finn snatched the fry out of Tessa's hand before dipping it into ketchup. "Mom told me I'll never have a boyfriend if I always smell like bull manure."

"I usually don't agree with Mom, but..." Dahlia scrunched up her nose. "If the boot fits."

Finn picked up an onion ring and threw it at Dahlia, hitting the bridge of her nose. Dahlia held up the soda spray hose from behind the bar, her finger hovering over the dispensing button. "Who needs a shower when I can hose you off right here, little sis?"

"Well, I'm going to go make a phone call before I get hit by friendly fire." Duke shoved his bar stool back before standing. "Carry on."

"Do *not* carry on, you two." Tessa cast a covert glance around the room to see who was watching their immature display. She shouldn't have been surprised to discover Grayson's eyes on her. After all, she'd felt the weight of his stare all evening—even when he was pretending to be preoccupied with securing the perimeter. Of course, it was hard to escape his attention when Tessa was sitting in front of the twelve-foot-long antique gilt-edged mirror that ran the length of the wall behind the bar.

"He's a serious one, huh?" Dahlia jerked her chin in Grayson's direction. "Does he ever take a break?"

"Not that I've seen so far." Tessa studied the labels on the long line of beers on tap. "Hey, Dia, for an old brothel-turned-speakeasy, you sure have done wonders with the place. Is that shiplap on the walls original to the building?"

"Yes! It was buried under layers of cheap wallpaper and cigar smoke, but I think it adds a sort of rustic charm."

"She got you." Finn shook her head at her twin. "Are we pretending to be on a home remodeling show now? Or can we go back to talking about Tessa's sexy bodyguard?"

"I'd prefer to talk about anything *but* that." Tessa hooked one of the heels from her borrowed boots in the rung of the bar stool.

"You have a lot of rules, big sister," Finn told her. "How are we supposed to have a conversation if we aren't allowed to talk about anything interesting?"

Tessa looked around for Duke, who normally called his husband on speakerphone so everyone could say hi. Where was the peacemaker when she needed him?

Just then, Violet Cortez-Hill walked in the front door. Violet had been in Teton Ridge for Roper King's funeral and, when MJ got arrested, Sherilee had hired her as his attorney.

Oh, and Violet used to be Marcus's girlfriend in high school. So Tessa definitely owed the woman for taking some of her family's attention off of her.

"Hey, Vi!" Dahlia came out from behind the bar to hug the newcomer. "I heard you were staying in town to help my baby brother out of his latest scrape with the law."

"Much to the annoyance of your *big* brother," Violet responded. "He isn't here, is he?"

"Not yet." Tessa smiled at the woman she'd once expected to be her sister-in-law.

Violet let out a deep breath as she plopped herself onto a gold-leather-covered bar stool. "In that case, I'll take a glass of any wine you already have open."

Dahlia drew a bottle from under the bar just as Freckles breezed out of the kitchen carrying two double burgers loaded with every possible topping listed on the limited bar menu.

"Hey, Aunt Freckles," Violet said. "If I had known you were here cooking, I would've left the courthouse earlier. Did Mrs. King kick you out of her kitchen?"

Violet hadn't dated Marcus in over fourteen years,

however, she apparently hadn't forgotten about the King family dynamics.

"No, darlin'." Freckles wore a crisp white apron over her tight zebra-printed blouse and even tighter jeans. "I needed a break from Rider. That old coot has been getting a bit frisky lately. Trying to prove there's still a little gas left in his tank, if you know what I mean."

Tessa and her two sisters all covered their ears, despite the fact that they should've been well accustomed to the older woman's candid comments.

"Aunt Freckles," Dahlia scolded as she lowered her cupped palms. "We can't unhear those sorts of things."

"You know what's crazy?" Finn asked, as though the last few days had been completely sane and normal. "Big Millie's used to be a place where men would come looking for female companionship. Yet now it's full of us trying to hide out from the men in our lives."

"Who says I'm hiding out from anyone?" Dahlia asked a bit too quickly, using a dishrag to scrub at an invisible spot on the bar. The way she refused to make eye contact with any of them made Tessa realize that something was going on with her sister.

And where had Duke gone? Was he hiding out from the man in his life, too? It was weird that Sherilee had pressured the Joint Chiefs of Staff to give Duke leave, but not Tom, who was also in the Navy.

Especially because Sherilee absolutely adored her son-in-law and got along with him better than several of her biological children. Of course, Tom was also a heart surgeon assigned to the hospital at Walter Reed and always kept an extra blood pressure cuff on hand to assure their mom that she wasn't going into cardiac arrest every time her kids stressed her out.

But before Tessa could subject her other siblings to the interrogation she'd just faced, Marcus's twin boys tore through the front door and ran straight for the billiards table. Their father was right behind them, still wearing his sheriff's uniform. His face was drawn tight, his lips pressed together. He was pissed about something and made a direct line toward Violet. Sensing another argument, Tessa and Finn stood, casually maneuvering themselves in front of their friend.

"Now you've got my sisters protecting you, too?" Marcus asked his ex-girlfriend.

"I only need protection from *credible* threats." Violet rose and stepped forward between Tessa and Finn. "And you, Sheriff King, are no threat."

Grayson appeared out of nowhere and asked, "Is everyone okay over here?"

"You know what this party needs?" Aunt Freckles clapped her hands together like a schoolteacher trying to get the attention of a rambunctious class. She pointed to the jukebox that was now playing a lively classic by George Straight. "Dancing!"

"No, thank—" Tessa's protest was cut off by a bony elbow to her ribs.

"Remember when I taught you kids how to do the two-step?" Freckles might be in her eighties, but the strong nudge at Tessa's back proved the woman was still a force of nature. "Tessa, you go ahead and show Agent Wyatt how to do it."

Grayson held up his hands in protest, which was a big mistake since a second shove from Freckles forced Tessa right into his arms. In an effort to steady herself, Tessa's palms landed on either side of his broad chest. She raised pleading eyes to his, but his irises had grown darker, his pectoral muscles flexing under her fingers.

"Finn, you go with Agent Doherty," Freckles continued, though Tessa was afraid to move her head even an inch to see if her sister complied. She didn't want to risk drawing even closer to Grayson. "And, Marcus, you and Violet can talk about whatever you need to talk about on the dance floor."

Tessa wanted to point out that there wasn't really a dance floor in Big Millie's, but her breath was caught in her throat. Agent Lopez and one of the other agents must've taken pity on the paired dancers because soon everyone who was off duty began moving in a circle across the wood-plank floors.

When she and Grayson remained in place, Freckles stepped up behind Tessa, creating a two-stepping sandwich that forced Tessa even closer to Grayson.

"Here, I'll show you again, darlin'. And step, step, slide. Step, step, slide."

It was either start dancing or be trampled by a determined eighty-something-year-old woman in high-heeled snakeskin cowboy boots.

"Sorry," Tessa muttered to Grayson, who looked more amused than annoyed by her aunt's high-handed antics. "Just get me to the other side of the bar and my aunt will find someone else to bug."

Surely, she and Grayson could stay close enough like this for a few seconds. Then Tessa would be able to get her breathing and her body temperature back under control.

Chapter Eight

Grayson was supposed to be off the clock. Instead of enjoying a long, mind-numbing run or a protein shake after an invigorating weight lifting session in the Kings' custom gym, he was steering Tessa around several tables in some old saloon in Middle of Nowhere, Wyoming.

At least Freckles had moved on to another couple in need of her dance instruction, or her peace-keeping skills in the case of Marcus and Mitchell Junior's attorney.

Grayson kept one hand on the curve of Tessa's waist and the other clasped around the soft skin of her delicate palm. However, making his legs move in sync with hers while still maintaining his space was a lot easier said than done.

"Maybe I should lead?" Tessa suggested after he nearly crashed them into an old-fashioned wooden barrel holding the billiard cues.

"I can do it," he said.

"You need to spin me or swing me or something. Make it look realistic. Otherwise, Aunt Freckles is going to insist we keep dancing until we get it right."

A groan reverberated in the back of his throat, sending a vibration through him. He could feel the heat from her body against his and didn't think he could last another song being this close to her. "Your family always seems to get what it wants."

"You know that expression 'failure isn't an option'?" she asked. He replied by spinning her to the right just in time to avoid a collision with Finn and Doherty, who were showing off some sort of pretzel maneuver in the middle of their path. "I think my family invented that expression."

"So nobody is allowed to fail? Or make mistakes?" he asked, thinking the code name Precision really suited her. Yesterday on the trail, she'd freely admitted that she hated being wrong. She'd also been overly concerned with what seemed to him like a mild stutter, and there was no telling how she'd react if that video footage of her lighting into Grayson in the staging tent was leaked. Even though he still stood by his decision and knew an inquiry board would likely vindicate him, he had no doubt that she wouldn't try to save her own reputation by portraying him to be the bad guy.

"It's not that," she replied. "Mistakes are okay as long as they make you better at winning."

Grayson slowed his steps, his eyes searching hers. "Have you ever *not* won, Tessa?"

She tried to look away, but their faces were too close. Finally, she sighed and he felt her warm breath along his neck. "I've lost something before."

"*Some*thing? Just one?" he asked. Tessa didn't respond for a few seconds. The song had changed to a slower one at some point, but their bodies were still swaying in time together. Not wanting to think about what was going on below their shoulders, he added, "Why do I feel like there's a story there?"

"Why do *I* feel like you could find out anything you wanted about me and probably already have?"

"I only know what I need to know as it pertains to the operation."

She made a scoffing sound, causing her chest to press against his. Heat spread through his rib cage. "That's right. I'm the operation. Not a person. Just a job for you."

"Were you hoping for something more?" He should've stepped back, put more distance between them. But he didn't want her to know how her nearness was affecting him. Hell, he didn't want to admit it to himself.

"Of course not." Crimson color flooded her cheeks and she was the one who took a step back. "It's just weird hearing someone else describe me that way. I mean, at the risk of sounding conceited, I'm used to people knowing about my life. Or at least thinking they know. It's one of the trade-offs of being the daughter of a famous man."

"And for being famous in your own right," he pointed out. "Or did you forget you're on TV every night? You're a reporter. Everyone knows who you are."

"I'm not a reporter. I'm a political analyst."

He raised an eyebrow. "Really? There's a difference?"

"Yes. But it seems like you already have your mind made up about that, too."

"It's not my job to make up my mind about anything. Like I said, my only objective is the operation. Digging for information about your personal life would've crossed one of those boundaries."

Unfortunately, the music cut off right before he said the last sentence. Even more unfortunately, Finn King and Doherty had danced their way right up next to them and overheard his words.

Finn looked down at his hand resting above the curve of her sister's hip. "You and Tessa both could stand to cross a few boundaries, if you ask me."

Doherty let out a bark of laughter and told his dance partner, "You have no idea."

Grayson quickly dropped his arms to his sides as though he'd just been touching a ticking time bomb. And in a way he had. He shouldn't have been socializing with the Kings, let alone dancing with one of them. Holding her body against his…

He cleared his throat. "I'm only following orders."

"Aunt Freckles's orders?" Finn quirked her eyebrow. "I didn't realize you worked for her."

Ouch. Grayson felt the reprimand like a punch to the gut. She was right, though. He didn't work for any of them.

"Leave him alone, Finn." Tessa frowned at her giggling sister, who easily spun away in Doherty's arms. She turned back to face him. "Ignore her, Grayson. You're off duty."

He shook his head. "I'm never off duty."

The words hung between them before he pivoted on his heel and walked toward the exit. He'd go and relieve one of the agents covering the door. The brisk night air would help to cool him down. Besides, getting back on the watch was the best way to ensure his guard didn't slip again.

Tessa tried not to think of the way her body had so easily slid against Grayson's last night when they'd been dancing at Big Millie's. She rarely drank socially—at least not since that party in college when she'd had a few too many and her speech had gotten a little too slurry—so she hadn't expected the craft beer to go to her head so quickly. That was the only reason why she'd allowed herself to dance so close to the sexy agent. The only reason why she'd let his words about her just being part of his operation provoke her into making him prove otherwise.

At least, that's what she told herself while she brushed her teeth the following morning.

Okay, so maybe she had been flirting with him a bit last night. Thankfully, he'd called her out on it, asking her if she'd been hoping for something more between them. Then Finn had come along and made that joke about them crossing boundaries and Grayson had switched right back into serious agent mode—which was what Tessa needed him to do.

One of them had to retain some sense of control.

Tessa waited until she knew both her mother and Aunt Freckles would be out of the kitchen before hunting down a cup of hot coffee so that she could feel slightly more human. A black SUV pulled up in the driveway, but before she could see who exited, Tessa scooped several newspapers off the kitchen table, and a freshly made cinnamon roll, and headed to her father's office. Thank goodness Roper King had always insisted on reading his news in print. She was less likely to run across a sensationalized picture of her in the black-and-white *Wall Street Journal* than she would online. And even though she was in a sense hiding out, Tessa still needed to stay sharp for her job.

The current events of today would likely be old news by tomorrow, and she wouldn't know what exactly she was looking for until she found it. But researching something—anything—gave her a sense of purpose and she always dove deep into anything she did.

After a few hours, though, the tiny letters on the pages started running together and her notes on the yellow pad beside her became impossible to decipher. Needing a break, Tessa took a couple of Tylenol to cut down on the pounding in her temples. She wasn't hungover from the night before, exactly, but she didn't think getting back on a horse today would do her head any favors.

Plus, she didn't want to risk having Grayson follow her again. Or worse, having him turn over the protective detail to another agent. That would mean that he was pissed off with her. It was a lose-lose situation, and the thought of losing always sent Tessa's nerves into overdrive.

Tessa grabbed a pair of sneakers and her wireless earbuds and set off on a run instead. She was only half a mile from the house when she realized that Grayson trailed behind her. Something fluttered inside her heart—or maybe she was just winded from her initial sprint up this hill. Either way, she turned up her music and pretended he wasn't there.

And for his part, he stayed a safe distance behind her.

Good, she told herself, picking up speed until she hit her stride. With each step she took, her thoughts cleared, her control returned. By the time she jogged back to the main house and showered, it was time for dinner with her family. Instead of engaging in the various arguments breaking out around the table, Tessa sipped her way through half a bottle of Cabernet, less worried about her speech slipping since she wasn't in public. In fact, she hadn't had to speak at all with all the voices spouting off around her. Wondering why Duke wasn't at dinner made her drink more.

Unfortunately, the wine and the constant bickering brought back her headache the following morning, and she repeated the same cycle as the day before.

Except, having exhausted her research on current events yesterday, she finally gave in and booted up her laptop. She began scrolling through her bookmarked online articles about traumatic brain injury until her head was swimming.

That afternoon, she set off on another run. Again, Grayson remained several yards behind. It didn't take long for a pattern to develop. For the rest of the week, any time she set off on a run or on a horseback ride—or even a quick trip on one of the ATVs to look at the southern fence line with Uncle Rider— the agent always stayed a respectable distance back.

A comfortable silence had settled between them, as though they were simply a pair of coworkers going about their jobs. It was a good reminder that Tessa was on duty, as well. She needed to work on her speech patterns and vocal exercises and stay abreast of everything else going on in the world. Luckily, fewer and fewer news headlines included her.

Until the day that she was returning to the stables on Phoebe and saw a black helicopter on the small helipad behind the bunkhouses. Grayson—who'd somehow managed to get Chandler to trust him again—raced ahead of her on his noble steed, as though he was going to throw his body in front of hers if so much as a single camera lens came into view.

This particular helicopter, though, wasn't some sightseeing charter for rent. It was an Airbus Super Puma, the cost way above the budget of most paparazzi and local news networks. It was also grounded, rather than being chased away by the fighter jets on standby. That meant whoever had landed it clearly wasn't a threat.

Still, Grayson held Tessa and Phoebe at a standstill by angling his horse right in front of the mare. Cupping a hand over his ear, he spoke to someone on the other end of his radio.

His eyes were hidden behind those damn sunglasses again, but she knew they were inspecting the area around them, taking in every potential threat. When he finally pivoted in his saddle to face her, his mouth was set in a grim line.

"It appears you have a visitor, Miss King."

Tessa's stomach sank. While Grayson hadn't said more than a handful of words to her since the night they'd danced at Big Millie's, none of them had been *Miss* or *King*. Or anything else quite as formal. Clearly, he was back to taking his role as protector way too seriously.

She was about to ask who the visitor was, but the front door of the main house opened and she didn't have to.

Davis Townsend. He'd called a few times since the pictures of her and Agent Steamy—*Agent Wyatt*, she mentally corrected herself—had come out. She'd called back once and ended up speaking to his personal assistant, who'd answered his phone. Then they'd only managed a few texts here and there. Tessa still hadn't formally rejected—or accepted—his proposal of marriage, so she shouldn't have been surprised that he would've flown out here expecting an answer.

"There you are, sweetheart!" he said as he approached Tessa and her horse. The woman she recognized as his press secretary was holding a smartphone at an odd angle, clearly prepared to capture a picture of what Davis probably planned as a loving reunion.

Tessa had been a part of politics for so long, she knew all the tricks. That was why she remained in the saddle, letting her horse walk in slow circles to cool down after the ride. "Davis? What are you doing here?"

"I had a break between town hall appearances and thought I'd surprise you." He planned to run for re-election for his district next November, but she knew he had his sights already set on the senatorial election coming up in two years.

"What's up with Debra?" Tessa jerked her chin toward his press secretary. "Didn't she get the memo about the ranch rules restricting camera access?"

"Oh that?" Davis looked back and gave a hand signal to the woman who quickly slipped her phone into her purse. "She must not have realized that applied to personal devices. After everything that's going on in the press, though, I understand you being hesitant about being photographed. Speaking of the press, I figured it's been long enough that I should come out here and put those rumors about you and that—" he hesitated "—bodyguard of yours to rest once and for all."

She snuck a peak at Grayson, whose stoic face didn't reveal that he'd just heard every word, even though he'd moved a few yards away and was maintaining a professional distance. At some point during the week, the agent had gotten a more suitable shirt—denim with snap buttons— and real boots. He could almost pass for an actual cowboy to the untrained eye.

Davis's eye, of course, was very untrained. Or,

as he often pointed out, he met so many people on the campaign trail, it was difficult for him to always put a name with a face. Sure, he could easily recognize the big donors, the top news executives and the political powerhouses. Yet, he could never remember the names of restaurant servers or event staff or even a few of his interns. A trait her father would've openly commented on if he'd witnessed it—and not favorably. She had no doubt that Davis was currently assuming that Grayson was just another cowboy working her family's ranch, which meant he wasn't worthy of a second glance.

Tessa swallowed her embarrassment on Grayson's behalf. "Davis, I'm sure you remember Agent Wyatt. Agent Wyatt, you already know Congressman Townsend."

"Of course." Grayson, who was still cooling down his own horse and probably had some sort of set of rules about shaking hands with anyone while he was on duty, barely nodded. "Although we weren't formally introduced last time."

"Last time?" Davis tilted his head, the confusion obvious along his very tanned brow. Was that bronzer?

"Feel free to refer to me as *that bodyguard.*" Grayson's face remained perfectly devoid of expression as he repeated the congressman's earlier description. "Or Agent Steamy. I'll answer to both."

"Aha!" Davis smiled his most charming smile,

as though he wasn't the least bit embarrassed to be called out on his mistake. "Forgive me, Agent Wyatt. I didn't recognize you out of uniform."

"Should I take the mare back to the stables for you, Miss King?" Grayson asked. He knew full well that she always insisted on being the one to give Phoebe her rubdown and oats after a ride.

"No, thanks," Tessa said, then turned to Davis. "I need to take care of my horse. You can wait for me at the main house if you want."

Davis's eyes darted between her and Grayson. He kept his smile in place, but Tessa sensed the jealousy vibrating in the air. After all, he'd already admitted that the only reason he was there was to put to rest the rumors about her with another man. Besides, having busy careers on opposite ends of the country meant that they were used to going months at a time without seeing each other. His being here after barely a week could mean only one thing. He was a desperate man making a desperate last-ditch attempt to maintain the appearance that all was well between them.

But it wasn't. And she couldn't—wouldn't—pretend.

"I'll help," Davis said and walked alongside her.

It was just as well, Tessa decided. She needed to put the man out of his misery once and for all.

She slid off her mare and loosened the cinch before leading her toward the stables, which housed almost one hundred horses at any given time. During herding season, which lasted from sunup to sundown, each cattle hand used at least two different horses a day so the animals weren't overworked.

Once inside, they passed the stock horses, the show horses and the trail horses. The rows of stalls were aptly named with little wooden signs Dahlia had once carved during summer camp. In addition to the Infirmary and Central Perk, there was also Shady Acres, a retirement community of sorts for horses of an advanced age, and Alcatraz, where they kept the animals that hadn't been amenable to riders or any sort of training—yet. Uncle Rider refused to ever give up on a horse.

"Is your bodyguard going to be within earshot of us the whole time?" Davis asked, jerking his head over to the grooming station at the other end of the row.

"He's a Secret Service agent, not a bodyguard. And his horse needs to be rubbed down, as well. If you don't want him here, you can offer to clean out Chandler Bing's hooves yourself."

Davis looked down at his well-manicured hands. "I just wanted a few minutes to ourselves so that we can talk about our announcement."

Tessa's stomach dropped. She really should've had this conversation with him earlier. But her father's funeral hadn't seemed like the appropriate time for the discussion and she hadn't wanted to do it over the phone or by text.

Complete the survey below and return it today to receive up to 4 FREE BOOKS and FREE GIFTS guaranteed!

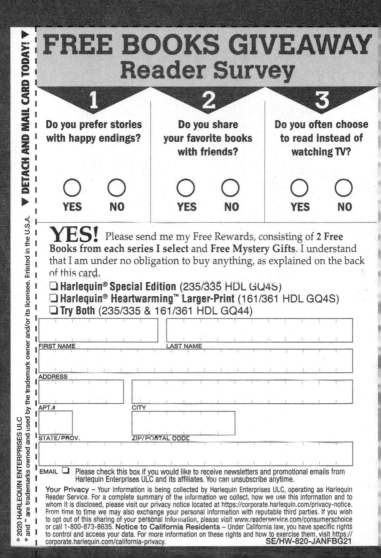

▼ DETACH AND MAIL CARD TODAY! ▼

FREE BOOKS GIVEAWAY
Reader Survey

1

Do you prefer stories with happy endings?

◯ YES ◯ NO

2

Do you share your favorite books with friends?

◯ YES ◯ NO

3

Do you often choose to read instead of watching TV?

◯ YES ◯ NO

YES! Please send me my Free Rewards, consisting of **2 Free Books from each series I select** and **Free Mystery Gifts**. I understand that I am under no obligation to buy anything, as explained on the back of this card.

❏ **Harlequin® Special Edition** (235/335 HDL GQ4S)
❏ **Harlequin® Heartwarming™ Larger-Print** (161/361 HDL GQ4S)
❏ **Try Both** (235/335 & 161/361 HDL GQ44)

FIRST NAME   LAST NAME

ADDRESS

APT.#   CITY

STATE/PROV.   ZIP/POSTAL CODE

EMAIL ❏ Please check this box if you would like to receive newsletters and promotional emails from Harlequin Enterprises ULC and its affiliates. You can unsubscribe anytime.

© 2020 HARLEQUIN ENTERPRISES ULC ● ® and ™ are trademarks owned and used by the trademark owner and/or its licensee. Printed in the U.S.A.

HARLEQUIN READER SERVICE—Here's how it works:

▼ If offer card is missing write to: Harlequin Reader Service, P.O. Box 1341, Buffalo, NY 14240-8531 or visit www.ReaderService.com ▼

BUSINESS REPLY MAIL

FIRST-CLASS MAIL   PERMIT NO. 717   BUFFALO, NY

POSTAGE WILL BE PAID BY ADDRESSEE

HARLEQUIN READER SERVICE
PO BOX 1341
BUFFALO NY 14240-8571

NO POSTAGE
NECESSARY
IF MAILED
IN THE
UNITED STATES

"What announcement?" Tessa asked, knowing full well exactly what he wanted to announce.

"Our engagement. I was going to fly my personal jeweler out here to the ranch, but your mother said there were some issues with your younger brother right now and the Secret Service had you guys on lockdown."

"That's right. I don't believe I saw your name on the original list of approved visitors." Probably because Tessa herself had been the one to strike his name from the list. Apparently, that had been the right call considering Davis had been going behind her back to plot with Sherilee.

"I'm a United States congressman, Tessa. The Secret Service works for m—the government," he corrected himself at the last second before looking over his shoulder to see if Grayson was within hearing range.

Interesting that he claimed his status as a congressman rather than his status as her boyfriend to explain why he should be there. But then again, she wasn't at all surprised.

"About that engagement, Davis." Tessa loosely tied the horse's reins to the edge of the watering trough before hefting the saddle off her. "You know, I never actually accepted your proposal."

There seemed to be very little in Tessa's life that she had control over at that exact moment, but she'd be damned if she was going to give up control over who she planned to marry. In fact, she was rather annoyed by Davis's arrogance in showing up unannounced and assuming otherwise.

"You never declined, either," he pointed out.

"I never really had time to respond at all," she said, although she'd been sitting out here on the ranch with absolutely nothing but time. Tessa ran her hands down Phoebe's legs, checking for possible injuries and swelling.

"So you want to wait longer before we get engaged," Davis stated rather than asked. She'd first met him when he'd been newly elected. When he'd been filled with bright ideas and shining promises, still fresh off the fight of a hard-won election. In the past two years, though, he'd eased into his position, and it was comfortable having a boyfriend who was just as busy as she was. A guy who didn't mind showing up on her arm for public appearances when their schedules allowed it, yet never insisted on going on actual dates or doing all those couple-type things that neither one of them had time for.

Somewhere along the way, though, Tessa had failed to notice the transition in his personality, the rise in his ego. Or perhaps she just hadn't cared because she too had been so absorbed in her own career. They were more like companions, or even colleagues, rather than significant others. When they were together, they talked about current events and their jobs and everything else but themselves. In fact, most of the things Davis knew about her could be found on her Wikipedia page. Grayson, after only a few days, already knew way more about Tessa than that. The sudden realization made it easier to finally say what had needed to be said for several months.

"No, I don't need to wait any longer." She pushed her shoulders back and faced him. "I'm not going to marry you, Davis."

"Is it because of him?" He jerked his head toward the other end of the aisle, where Grayson was hosing down his horse.

"No, I should have told you when you first asked. I let things go on too long and…well, like I said, there never seemed to be any good time."

"But what about the media reports? All the speculation and gossip is going to haunt my upcoming reelection bid."

An unexpected chuckle burst out of her throat. "The fact that you're more concerned with your reelection bid than with a broken heart is evidence that you never really loved me in the first place."

"People like us are too busy for love, Tessa. Sure, a big romance might make for a nice story, but there're more important things than that. Like our careers. Besides, being together makes sense. We get along and we run in the same circles. Really, it's a win-win for both of us. You're the brainy one with the family connections and I'm the charming one with the people skills," he said, not realizing how utterly uncharming he sounded at that exact moment. "Together, we could've gone farther than Roper King could have ever hoped."

Her stomach turned over. She knew their relationship had mostly been based on appearances, but she'd thought there'd been at least a mutual respect there, as well. It shouldn't have surprised her that she was just a step on his career ladder. A big step, but a step nonetheless.

"My dad got exactly as far as he wanted, Davis. And, for the record, he hated people who needed to use someone else to get ahead."

"I was never using you." His eyes narrowed into angry slants. "At least, not any more than you were using me."

"How did I use you?" she asked, crossing her arms at her chest. "I'd love to hear this."

"Tessa King had the reputation of being a cold, cutthroat bitch before I came along. I humanized you. Being in a relationship with me made you at least seem like a real woman."

The urge to deliver a cutting remark threatened to choke her, but she refused to give him the satisfaction of reacting to his stinging insult. Instead she replied in her most dismissive tone. "I think you need to leave now, Congressman Townsend."

"But your mother invited me—"

"Miss King has politely asked you to leave." Grayson had made it to their side of the stables in less than two seconds. "I'll have the command center radio your pilot so you can fly out of here on your own accord."

"Or else what?" Davis's chin lifted.

"Or else we can escort you from the premises in the backseat of the Ridgecrest County Sheriff's patrol unit." Marcus's commanding voice came from out of nowhere.

No, not nowhere. Her brother walked out from an empty stall followed by Violet, her dark hair flecked with several strands of dried hay. Tessa would've asked them what they'd been doing if her brother's eyes weren't so filled with fury.

"Before you make your choice," Marcus continued, "it's only fair to warn you that my squad car doesn't have tinted windows. I'm sure the press stationed outside the gates would love to get a great shot of you back there."

Davis took a step in retreat and flashed that ridiculous fake grin again. "We're good. I was just leaving."

The congressman walked away, with Marcus and Violet following a few feet behind. Marcus probably because he wanted to make sure Davis actually left, and Violet probably because she didn't want anyone asking her what she was doing inside one of the stalls with her ex-boyfriend.

When they were out of sight, Tessa felt the air rush out of her lungs. She smoothed a hand over the mare's damp coat, trying not to notice the slight tremble in her fingers.

"Are you okay?" Grayson's voice was low, his body suddenly close.

"I'm fine." Tessa sniffed and pushed her hair back from her flushed face, sounding anything but composed. "Davis was upset, but it wasn't like I needed you guys to jump in and save me. I wasn't in any danger."

"Then why are you shaking?" Of course Grayson would notice. He was always too damn observant. She dropped her hand and turned to him.

"Because I'm mad at myself for not ending things sooner. I never should've al...al...allowed—" She forced the word out, but the effort made her close her eyes. She put her tongue on the roof of her mouth and counted to five, but the sound of the helicopter's engine, followed by the slow churn of the propeller, saved her from having to finish her sentence.

She turned back to brushing Phoebe, concentrating on the smooth strokes until the mare stomped her foot as though to say, *Enough. Take me back to my stall so I can get away from you crazy humans and eat.*

After caring for her horse, Tessa turned to the mundane tasks of cleaning the bit and bridle, reorganizing a row of leather reins in the tack room and even polishing the saddle.

"I'm pretty sure he's gone now," Grayson said

from the door of the tack room. "You don't have to keep hiding out in the stable."

"I'm not hiding from Davis Townsend." Tessa rolled her shoulders in circles to loosen the tension she couldn't seem to shake. When Grayson kept staring at her, she finally sighed. "Everyone but my mom has been predicting our breakup for a year now. I didn't want to give any of them the satisfaction back then. So now I'm hiding out from my family and all their I-told-you-sos. Plus, I'm so damn mad at my mother for inviting him out here in the first place, I need to cool down before I say anything I might regret."

"How long will that take?" he asked, looking at his watch.

"Probably a few weeks." She yanked the elastic band from her hair and massaged her scalp. "Look, you don't have to stay here and babysit me. If you're off duty, you can go do…whatever you do in your free time."

"I'm never—"

"Yeah, I get it." She rolled her eyes as she cut him off. "You're never off duty."

He smirked, the rare quasi smile suddenly making him seem less like a robot. Tessa had a sudden urge to see the man relax for a change and let down his guard.

"I'm going to make your job easy then, Agent Wyatt. Mr. Truong, our stable manager, keeps a cold six-pack of beer in the back of the tiny fridge in his office. I'm going to go borrow a couple of bottles, along with the keys to one of the ATVs. Then I'm taking a joyride up to Pine Top Point. You can either go back to the bunkhouse and recruit another agent to trail me, or you can go back to the bunkhouse to see if you can find us a bag of chips and maybe some of those homemade sandwiches Aunt Freckles keeps sending out to you guys by the trayful. Either way, I'm leaving here in five minutes with or without you."

Chapter Nine

Technically, he'd gotten off duty halfway through the horse ride. But Grayson hadn't been about to leave Tessa alone with that blowhard fiancé of hers. In fact, after Davis Townsend had left, Grayson found reasons to hang around the stables, telling himself that he was remaining on standby, just in case Tessa needed him for something. Even if it was only to vent.

But she hadn't broken down crying or gone on a rampage or done any of the other things he would've expected a woman to do if the man she loved had just called her a cold, cutthroat bitch. Personally, Grayson had wanted to shove his fist in the guy's face, but had to settle for diplomatically telling the jerk to get lost.

In fact, Tessa hadn't seemed all that bothered by the breakup. Judging by that accidental stutter, she'd been more embarrassed than anything else.

Clearly, she hadn't needed Grayson to swoop in and rescue her. Nor had she needed the comfort of her family, who most definitely would've given her a hard time about not dumping "Congressman Smooth" sooner. Tessa had simply wanted to get away from all the drama.

So then why was he currently clinging to the roll bar of the two-seater ATV as she raced along the dirt trail that wound up to Pine Top Point?

Maybe because he just simply needed to get away from his job, too.

As she hastily shifted gears tearing along the rutted path, he felt himself slowly shift from the role of agent to the role of...friend? No, not friend, he corrected himself when Tessa hit a large rock in the road and sent them skidding sideways before regaining control of the steering wheel. Advisor.

"Are you sure you don't want me to drive?" he yelled above the revving engine as she took another steep incline at Mach 4.

"No. Just hold on to the beer and make sure none of the bottles fly out."

It was hard to hold on to the beer when he also had to brace himself from slamming his head against the roll bar. These jacked-up golf carts weren't made for men his size.

When they finally reached the top of the trail, Tessa shut off the engine but left the keys in the ignition. Grayson waited until she'd climbed out of the driver's seat before slipping the keys into his pocket. The sun would be setting in less than an hour and there was no way he was letting her drive down the hill in the dark.

"Thanks for bringing the food," she said as she grabbed the bag of sandwiches from the metal lockbox strapped to the back of the vehicle.

"I didn't have time to wrap them up, so if it looks like someone lost a cafeteria food fight in there, you can blame that on your refusal to stay on the road."

"We're on a ranch, Grayson. Roads and trails are only suggestions out here." She weaved her way through a wall of overgrown fir trees. "Come on, we have to hike the rest of the way."

He caught up to her quickly and, after winding through fifty yards or so of trees, the peak of the mountain gave way to a flat grassy spot and the most amazing view he'd ever seen.

"Whoa," he said, suitably impressed. "You can see the whole ranch from up here."

Or at least the western half of it. The sun was sinking behind the Teton mountain range in the distance and the sky couldn't seem to decide if it wanted to be purple, pink or orange.

She set down the bag of food and then surprised him by plopping herself cross-legged onto the cold ground without so much as a blanket between the long grass and her designer jeans.

Don't think about her jeans, he reminded himself.

Tessa reached up a hand and his first thought was that she was going to grab onto him and pull him down beside her. It wasn't until she asked, "Do you mind sharing one of those?" that he realized she was reaching for a beer.

"Sorry," he said, shoving the cardboard case at her.

She set the six-pack on the grass and twisted off the top of one before passing the open bottle to him. "Are you ever allowed to sit down on the job?"

He hadn't officially been on the job for the past three hours. He'd even left his earpiece and his duty weapon back in the bunkhouse. Otherwise, he never would have accepted the beer. But there was a hand-held radio in the ATV, along with an emergency kit and a holstered rifle mounted inside the lockbox— just in case they ran into an unfriendly bobcat or grizzly bear. So as long as he had only one drink, he was still well within regulations.

Just to be safe, though, he sat a few feet away from Tessa, careful to keep the bag of food and the remaining six-pack between them. They were lucky they'd caught a break with this unusual warm weather—or at least warm for Wyoming in January. All the snow had melted and they weren't expecting more for another week or so.

He racked his brain for something to talk to her about that didn't include the off-limit subjects. Normally, Grayson could sit in the quiet for hours, but that was when he was working. Right now—he took a sip of the craft beer that wasn't quite as cold as when they'd set out—he was off the clock.

Grayson preferred to operate in terms of black and white, however, being around Tessa King was like being surrounded by every color in between.

His mind struggled with the distinction, with those boundary lines of being on the job and off the job. On duty meant suits, eating on the go and conversations with Doherty on his radio earpiece. Off duty meant sunsets, beer and making conversation with pretty women. He took another long gulp, then leaned back on his hands, taking in the incredible view.

"So." Tessa finally broke the silence. "In the past week, you've pretty much seen me at all my worst moments."

"I thought you didn't want to talk about the breakup. Or your family," he added.

"You're right," she said, then lifted the bottle to her lips. His own mouth went dry and he forced himself to look away. "So let's talk about you."

"Or we could talk about your job," he suggested,

thinking he would lead her into a neutral subject that would interest her.

"We could," she answered. "But I'm more interested in finding out about your family. What's Maddie like?"

The unexpected question took Grayson aback. He was so accustomed to people focusing on Maddie's medical condition, it was almost jarring when they wanted to know about her as a person.

"Well... She's smart. Like, wicked smart. She loves art, making it and studying it. In fact, she's working on getting her online degree in art history. She loves candy and Jane Austen books and all of the Rocky movies. She once wrote an English paper about how *Rocky* was the ultimate love story and the boxing was only secondary to the plot."

Tessa laughed. "I'd have to agree with her there."

Grayson shook his head but continued since he was on a roll. "Maddie's witty and sarcastic and nosy as hell. But she's also kind and caring and loves giving advice. Even when it's unsolicited."

"Like what? Give me an example of her unsolicited advice."

He immediately thought of his sister's comment that he needed someone and hadn't really dated since his divorce. But he didn't feel like sharing that with Tessa. So instead he said, "She thinks I work too hard."

Tessa's grin widened. "I'd have to agree with her on that, as well."

"Says the woman who rarely takes a day off. Even when you're supposed to be relaxing on the ranch, I know you're still spending a lot of time in your father's study behind that computer screen."

"I've got to stay sharp on current events. The rest of the world is still going on out there without me. When I return to work, I've got to be ready to jump right back in and hit the ground running."

Grayson respected her for her dedication, but felt a weird sensation zip through him at the reminder that she'd be going back to work soon. He took a drink to wash the feeling away, then asked, "How'd you decide you wanted to be a political analyst?"

"Well, it wasn't my original career choice." She took another drink.

"Yeah, I think I read somewhere that you were training for the Olympics at one point."

"You can't believe everything you read." She gave a half-hearted smirk; her reference to the reason why they were still in Wyoming wasn't lost on him. "But I don't want to talk about that, either."

"Then let's eat," he suggested, because at this point he was out of conversation topics and he was getting hungry. Plus, he knew better than to drink on an empty stomach.

He rummaged around in the bag and pulled out two different brands of chips. Then he tore the brown paper along one side, turning the bag into a giant place mat. "Your choices are a turkey and Swiss on wheat—or at least partially on wheat since the contents shifted midflight. Or there's a roast beef and cheddar on some sort of roll. I can't tell under all that mustard."

"Gotta go for the mustard," she said, taking the foil-wrapped package smeared with the yellow condiment.

He dug in to the turkey sandwich while she only took a few bites before setting hers down. She licked her fingers and Grayson almost groaned before shoving his remaining food into his mouth and shifting a few more inches away.

Tessa cracked open another bottle, took a small sip and then asked, "Have you ever gone through a public breakup, Grayson?"

A knot formed below his sternum and he wished he hadn't eaten quite so fast. He swallowed the rest of his beer to wash everything down before answering. "I haven't ever done anything publicly. I keep my private life private."

He hadn't meant the words to be an insult, but her lips tightened all the same. "Fair enough. How about a regular breakup? Ever been through one of those?"

He sucked in a breath, twisting the bottle in his hands, unsure of how much or how little he should say.

Apparently, he must've taken too long to answer

because she suddenly gasped. "Oh my gosh! I don't even know if you're married or not."

As much as he wanted to keep things professional between them, Grayson couldn't deny that there was a mutual attraction. If she was thinking about him in all the same ways he was thinking about her, then it wouldn't be fair to let her believe she was lusting after someone else's husband.

"No." He shook his head, keeping his gaze straight ahead. "I haven't been married for a long time."

"But you were. That means your breakup must've been a way bigger deal than the little falling-out you witnessed back at the stables." She paused, as though she was waiting for him to agree. But before he could respond, she caught her breath again, her eyes going wide. Reaching across the remains of their picnic, she clasped his forearm. Even through the canvas material of his borrowed work coat, he felt the heat of her touch. Her voice was full of concern when she said, "Unless your wife passed away. I'm so sorry if—"

"No," he said a bit too abruptly then cleared his throat. "Nothing as tragic as that."

He took another drink of his beer, mostly so that he had a reason for breaking their physical contact. But the crinkled lines above Tessa's nose meant she wasn't quite convinced he didn't have some sort of sob story to tell. And the determined gleam in her eyes meant she wasn't going to stop asking questions until he offered up something.

Grayson shrugged. "My ex-wife was a nurse. One of Maddie's nurses, in fact. Jamie quit her job, though, when I got stationed overseas, so she could come with me. She wanted children right away, but I wasn't ready. I figured we should have plenty of money saved up so that when kids came, we could pay for anything they might need."

"That's understandable, considering…"

"My sister's medical needs," Grayson finished for her. "That was the other half of the equation. Not only were we living off just my paycheck, I also needed to send money home to my mom and Maddie. I was never a big spender, so it rarely crossed my mind that I should be using my money for anything besides the bare necessities.

"After a while, though, Jamie resented the fact that we were going without so that I could keep sending money home. I explained that it didn't seem fair for me to go out for a good time, living it up, when my sister was stuck in a bed or a wheelchair most of the time. Not that it was fair to Jamie, either, I guess. Although, she knew going into the marriage that I'd promised my dad to always look after my sister."

"Your dad passed away?"

"Yes. When I was still in high school."

"I'm sorry." Tessa reached her hand across to his arm again. This time, Grayson held still, trying to ignore the comforting warmth. He'd rather talk about his divorce than the loss of his father, so he returned to the story.

"Anyway, there was a new medication on the market that I thought would help Maddie. But her insurance wouldn't cover the monthly cost, which was about the same amount we were paying for rent.

"Jamie, being in the medical field, thought the medication wouldn't work anyway and would end up being a waste of money. We had a huge fight. She didn't appreciate the fact that I couldn't afford to take her out to dinner because I was using all my overtime pay on trial medications and horseback riding lessons. And I couldn't really blame her. She was putting her life on hold so that I could take care of my sister. Not that I ever asked her to give up her job, but I guess she realized that Maddie would always be my priority over everything else. We parted ways, and…" Grayson shrugged. "Last I heard, she remarried several years ago and has a couple of kids now. So things worked out for the best."

He felt the weight of Tessa's stare as she studied him. A bird chirped from one of the trees in the distance; otherwise the air was thick with their silence. Then he heard a rustling sound and looked down to see that she'd moved the remaining chip bags to the other side of her so she could scoot closer.

"Thank you." Tessa patted his upper arm the way a friend would console another friend. After a few extra pats, she moved her hand up to his shoulder and gave him a reassuring squeeze. Grayson tried not to think about the electrical current that followed the same path. Or the way there was suddenly fewer beers and fewer feet between them.

"For reminding you that things will work out for the best?" he asked, trying to stay perfectly still despite her body leaning closer to him. Her palm absently made slow circles between his shoulder and his biceps.

"No, for sharing a part of yourself with me. I know it goes against the rules about mixing your professional life with your personal life. Whenever I'm around you, I always feel like my life is such a mess, while you're so perfect and calm and in control. It's nice to know that you're a human just like the rest of us."

"Tessa." Grayson's voice was low and tight in his throat. "If you keep stroking my arm like that, you're going to find out exactly how human I am."

Tessa recognized the hunger in Grayson's eyes. It matched the desire whirlpooling through her own bloodstream. The muscles in his biceps flexed under her palm and instead of pulling away, she trailed her fingers along the coiled ridges until she got to his sculpted shoulder.

Just a few more seconds, she told herself as her hand memorized the contours of his upper arm under his thin jacket. That's right. They were both wearing jackets. They were fully dressed. It wasn't like she was actually having skin-to-skin contact with…

Oh hell. Somehow, Tessa had maneuvered herself closer because her fingers were now brushing against the warm skin of his neck. Grayson's nostrils flared slightly, but he remained perfectly still as she pivoted toward him, her leg brushing against his. When had she risen to her knees? Had she crawled over to him? Was she that desperate to touch the man?

She couldn't gauge how much distance she'd closed between them because she didn't dare break eye contact. Their faces were only inches apart, his steel-gray gaze practically daring her to move in even closer. Her heart thumped frantically behind her rib cage as she accepted the challenge.

Tessa traced her thumb from his neck to his jaw, stopping just below the curve of his bottom lip. Grayson lifted his hand to her hip, but instead of pushing her away, he held on tighter.

"Tessa," he said so low, so deep, it sounded like more of a growl than a warning.

Her entire body was buzzing with anticipation. Of what, she didn't know. Tessa hadn't felt this alive since her last free-fall dive.

She sucked in a ragged breath, telling herself, *Just a little more.* After all, the whole point of her staying on the ranch in the first place was to ensure that she could handle her physical responses in emotionally charged situations. Was there a bigger test than right this second? A more perfect opportunity to prove to herself and to Grayson that she was in complete control? For just a few more seconds. Long enough for her to get a little bit closer…

Tessa brought her left knee over his lap, boldly straddling him, silently daring him the same way he'd dared her. Both of his hands captured her hips, his fingers digging into the soft flesh under her jeans.

"Grayson?" she asked.

His mouth was so near, she could feel the heat of his breath as he responded. "Yeah?"

"My life is about to get messy again," she warned before molding her lips to his.

She angled her face slightly before taking the kiss deeper, inviting his tongue to explore her mouth. And, oh how he explored everything she offered. He gripped her hips tighter, positioning her directly over his arousal, and then pulled her against him. Pleasure skimmed the surface of the juncture between her thighs and she ached to feel more. He wrapped one arm around her waist, holding her in place while his other hand trailed up her flannel shirt, his thumb easily slipping the buttons free until she felt the cool air whisper against her overheated skin.

She gasped, causing his mouth to break free long enough to blaze a path of hot kisses down her neck and toward her breasts. His thumb edged the lace of her bra lower until one of her tightened nipples sprung free. Grayson's tongue darted out and Tessa's fingers shot through his short brown hair, holding on for dear life as she threw back her head and moaned.

Heat surged through her core and she pressed herself closer to his hardened length.

Grayson groaned before tearing his mouth away from her exposed breast. "Tessa," he said, his breath coming out in short bursts. "We have to stop."

"I know," she agreed before reclaiming his lips under hers. *Just one more kiss*, she told herself as she surrendered to his skilled tongue again.

His hands framed her face and he gave her lower lip a final nip before easing her away from him a second time. Luckily, the sun had already set, making it easier to mask her disappointment. However, Tessa sensed that the growing darkness would soon give way to growing regret. Especially because in her effort to prove that she was in control, she'd totally lost control.

Her attempt to school her expression was wasted, though, since he was busy making quick work of returning her buttons to their proper holes. Grayson Wyatt, taking charge again. Although, this time it was for the best since her fingers were trembling too much to get the job done.

If she couldn't be in charge of her emotions, then she would have to settle for being in charge of the conversation.

"Don't you dare say something about crossing

some sort of professional boundary," she warned before peeling herself off him and rising.

"It also crosses an ethical boundary. You just broke up with your boyfriend. You were vulner—"

"Stop right there." She held up her hand. "Don't even say that word. I'm not weak, Grayson. I don't need to be protected or coddled. And I'm certainly not in mourning for a relationship that was already broken."

Dang. Mourning was the wrong word to use in this situation and he immediately seized upon it. "But you are still grieving your father."

"True. Although, there's something about our physical connection, about the way my body responds to you, that reminds me that I'm still very much alive. And don't deny that your body wasn't responding just as much to me."

He stood, his jaw tense, his jacket on the ground in a crumpled heap behind him. Tessa barely remembered sliding the outer layer off his shoulders. She only remembered her need to touch as much of him as possible.

"My body should be better trained than that, though." He dragged a hand through his hair, which she'd properly mussed only a few moments ago. "I love my job. Normally, I'm pretty damn good at it when there's not a beautiful and witty woman outrunning me on her horse. Getting involved with you while I'm on assignment is a distraction I can't afford."

Tessa shoved her hands into her back pockets, causing her still aching breasts to thrust forward. While she understood his position and even respected it, a tiny thrill shot through her at his admission. "So I'm a distraction?"

He stepped toward her then gently tucked a strand of hair behind her ear, allowing his thumb to linger against her cheek. "The very best kind. But to do my job well, I have to be thinking clearly at all times. You and your family deserve me at my best. No matter how much I want to strip off every single article of clothing you're wearing and see the real woman underneath, the fact remains that I'm on assignment right *now*."

A shiver of delight raced along her spine and she smiled at him, a challenge forming on her lips. "That implies that there will come a time when you aren't on duty. A time when this assignment is over."

"When that time comes, Miss King, there won't be a couple of layers of denim between us. I'll lie back and let you call all the shots." Grayson's promise caused a fluttering sensation deep within her belly. He picked up his coat and dug the keys out of his pocket. "But in the meantime, I'm in the driver's seat."

Chapter Ten

A week went by with Grayson and Tessa pretending that nothing had happened between them up at Pine Top Point. He thought he'd done a pretty good job of returning to business as usual. He'd even kept a straight face when Doherty asked why the new shirt Grayson had been wearing that night was missing two buttons.

Despite a slight surge of reporters the day after Congressman Townsend left, there were fewer and fewer white vans camped outside the gates. It could have had something to do with Duke King returning to his ship after his leave ended. With all those late-night phone calls on the front porch, the most levelheaded member of the King family definitely had something he wasn't sharing with his siblings. Perhaps the press had caught wind of it and followed him in search of a bigger story.

In fact, if things remained this quiet, they wouldn't need as many agents stationed on the ranch any longer. That meant Grayson could finally be done with *Operation Snowball*.

He was passing the stables on his way to the bunkhouse on a Tuesday afternoon when he caught a glimpse of Tessa heading out for her daily ride, a task that Grayson had ensured one of the other agents now covered. As much as his body was aching to be alone with her, his brain was telling him that he couldn't risk a repeat of that crazy make-out session last week.

"You can't ride the horses today," Finn yelled as she came tearing out of the stables, nearly mowing down Grayson in her attempt to reach her sister.

"Why not?" Tessa asked.

"The vet is finishing up the inoculations."

Grayson hadn't seen a veterinarian here earlier. That kind of information would've been on the visitor's log at the command center, where he'd just gotten off duty. Had his team missed something? The last thing he wanted to do right now was to stop and listen to their conversation, but there was no other agent around to confirm things and his investigation senses were tingling.

Tessa lifted a brow. "*All* the horses?"

Her sister looked over her shoulder at the entrance to the stables, probably hoping nobody came out to refute her lie. "It makes it easier to keep them all on the same yearly schedule for shots."

"Ugh!" Tessa stretched her arms over her head. "Mom keeps following me around with an open laptop and asking me when I'm ready to have a video conference with her public relations team. She's insisting that I make a statement to the press before Davis puts his own spin on our breakup. I need somewhere to hide out."

"You want to go to Big Millie's instead?" Finn managed to steer Tessa toward the house.

"I've been there almost every night the past week," Tessa argued. "Except for Thursday when Dahlia closed early for personal reasons and I babysat Amelia for her. Our niece insisted she had a new dog, but I think she was imagining it. Or maybe *I'm* imagining things. Either way, I'm going stir-crazy out here. I think it's time for me to go back to work."

"Have you been cleared by the neurolo—" Finn clamped her lips closed when Tessa gave her a very pointed look and then not so subtly darted her eyes in Grayson's direction.

Now, that was interesting, he thought to himself. Was Tessa under the care of a neurologist? As far as he knew, there'd been no doctors—animal or human—on the ranch in the past week.

Freckles chose that exact instant to walk out onto the front porch. Although, from what Grayson had observed of the older woman these past couple of weeks, she'd probably been standing behind the front door all along, strategically planning her entrance into the conversation. "You know, Tessa, your uncle tells me there's a new state-of-the-art indoor pool over at the rec center. I hear there's a diving board and everything."

Grayson was close enough that he could see the goose bumps rise above Tessa's wrists. "I'm not going diving, Aunt Freckles."

Yep. Aunt Freckles and Finn were definitely up to something.

"Of course you aren't. I was just thinking you could go do some laps. I'm sure Agent Grayson here and his team could call ahead to the rec center and get you a couple of hours by yourself."

No, Agent Grayson here wanted to get back to the bunkhouse and take a nap before he covered the night shift for Lopez. He certainly didn't want to stand by and watch Tessa King wearing nothing but a skimpy swimsuit as her athletic body glided through the water.

However, an hour later, before he was about to get behind the wheel of the black SUV, Freckles grabbed his elbow and whispered in his ear, "Try to get our girl up on the diving board."

Our girl was sitting in the backseat, her face devoid of expression. Only the subtlest clench of her jaw told him that she was upset about something—probably about the fact that she'd once again allowed herself to be cajoled by Finn and Freckles into doing something she was avoiding. Even though he was curious about whatever it was she wanted to avoid, Grayson was determined to keep his distance.

Two other agents rode along in the vehicle with them, so at least he wasn't alone with her. When they arrived at the local rec center, which, thankfully, had already been closed to the public for the evening, Grayson and Doherty went in first to clear and secure the H-shaped building. The main entrance and locker rooms were in the center of the H, the gymnasium running the length of one of the sides and the indoor pool running the length of the other. The only way to access the pool was through the locker room hallway or through the reception area. There was no rear exit, which made it easier for surveillance but more difficult if they needed to get out of there in an emergency.

Not that anyone was anticipating an emergency at some community rec center in the middle of Wyoming. Grayson rocked back on his heels, shaking off another wave of restlessness. Not every assignment could be action-packed and heart-stopping, he reminded himself.

"Indoor pools give me the creeps," Doherty said after they radioed Agent Talib to advise her that it was clear to bring Tessa inside. "It's unnatural to have this much water under a roof. It smells like weird chemicals and everything echoes in there. I'm going to post up by the front entrance."

Agent Talib was already in place outside the locker rooms to make sure nobody came in through that entrance, which meant Grayson got stuck inside the pool area with Tessa, the scent of chlorine permeating the dense air.

The lights were bright, buzzing overhead as Tessa lapped through the water. She swam a few lengths then stopped at the deep end and lifted her goggles onto her slicked-back hair. "You don't have to stand there the whole time watching me."

"I'm not *watching* you," he pointed out. "I'm scanning the area for possible threats. Sorry if you occasionally come into my field of vision."

"Right." Tessa adjusted her goggles, but not before he saw her roll her eyes. "Well, when you used to watch me on my rides, you'd actually get on a horse and pretend to at least be participating in the activity."

"I can't scan for potential threats from inside the pool."

"Please. We're in an enclosed room with no windows." Tessa used a dripping arm to gesture around the four tall walls surrounding the Olympic-size pool. "The only way in here is past the other two agents stationed at the doors. Do you really have that little confidence in your colleagues?"

"Someone has to remain inside. Besides, you shouldn't swim alone without a lifeguard on duty."

"Then swim *with* me." Using her open palm, she sent a spray of water his way.

"I didn't bring a suit," Grayson argued.

"Grab one from the lost and found." She pointed to a large metal-wire bin in the far corner.

He scrunched his nose. "That sounds pretty unhygienic."

She easily pulled herself out of the deep end, water sluicing from her body as her wet feet slapped along the deck. Her voice echoed off the tiled walls as she walked toward the lost and found bin. "Don't worry. The gallons of chlorine they dump in here will kill off any potential germs."

Germs were suddenly the last thing on his mind as he got a full look at Tessa King's toned legs, which were bare and slick all the way up to the blue spandex material barely covering the firm rounded curves of her backside. His throat went dry.

Tessa, hopefully oblivious to his body's reaction to her in a swimsuit, grabbed a pair of neon-green shorts boasting a wild print of frothy piña colada drinks and pink umbrellas. She held them up triumphantly as she made her way back to him.

Grayson shook his head. "Those look like they

were purposely left behind on a Hawaiian cruise ship by a retired NFL linebacker."

"Hmm." She squinted through one eye as she tested out the elasticity of the waistband, looking from the shorts to Grayson's lower torso. "Might be a few sizes too big. I think I saw a Speedo in there that would work better—"

He snatched the swim trunks out of her hand. "I'll make you a deal. I'll wear these ridiculous things— the Speedo is a no-go—if you teach me how to dive."

Grayson knew there was a reason Freckles had mentioned the diving board, and he wanted to find out why. Even if it meant sacrificing his pride and donning the tacky swim trunks, their obnoxiously bright print making him suddenly wish he had his sunglasses.

Tessa's eyes shot to the high dive and he saw the muscles in her neck working as she gulped. Yep, there was definitely a story there. She wrung the water out of her hair, but not before he saw the telltale twitch of her fingers. "What do you mean *teach* you how to dive? The great Agent Wyatt doesn't already know how to do something?"

Of course he knew how to dive. It was part of the combat swimmer stroke course when he'd trained for special forces. But if she didn't already know the details of his training, he wasn't going to volunteer the info. "My mom used to take me and Maddie swimming when we were growing up because it helped Maddie with her physical therapy. But our neighborhood pool didn't have fancy diving boards like these."

That was true enough. Maybe it was his subtle reminder of his sister having a medical condition. Or maybe Tessa just really wanted to see him shirtless. Or maybe she really felt awkward with him watching her while she swam alone. Either way, she inhaled deeply and stuck out her hand to shake on the deal. "Fine."

As he walked into the locker room to change, he explained to Agent Talib in passing that he wouldn't have his radio earpiece in for a short time. She'd replied, "Take as long as you want. I told SAIC Simon we didn't need three agents for this job, but Doherty insisted that you'd want to come along as an extra."

Damn, he thought, cinching the drawstring in the waistband and double knotting it to keep the swimsuit in place. Doherty had likely been in on this plan with Finn and Freckles all along.

When Grayson walked out of the locker room, Tessa was back in the pool, treading water. Her goggles were on the deck where she'd left them, which meant that when he approached in his borrowed suit, there was nothing to obscure her eyes as they widened at the sight of his bare chest.

She bit her lower lip, blatantly staring at the area below his neck. His skin tightened over his already tense muscles and heat spread through his blood-stream.

This is a bad idea. He didn't trust himself around her when they were both fully dressed. How could they be this close to each other in nothing but their swimsuits and keep their hands to themselves?

Unfortunately, it was too late to turn back now. He jumped into the water in an effort to cool off his overheated body and almost lost his shorts.

"Okay—" he nodded toward the board "—show me how to dive."

"You said 'teach,' not show. You go up on the springboard and I'll stay down here and talk you through it."

He should've known that she'd try to outsmart him. He used the side ladder and only one arm to haul himself out of the pool, the other hand still clutching the loose elastic of his shorts. Grayson walked onto the end of the diving board, prepared to belly flop on this whole plan if he had to.

Tessa gave him several instructions of how he should lean over at the waist or bend his knees or move his toes closer to the edge, but he purposely misunderstood everything she said and ended up jackknifed as he tumbled into the water.

The second time he got up on the board, he over-corrected and actually *did* do a belly flop. The red skin on Grayson's stomach stung as he walked back to the board for the third time. He swallowed his pride, along with his penchant for honesty, when he said, "I just don't understand what I'm doing wrong."

His first two attempts had taken so long, she'd given up on treading water in the deep end and was now sitting on the edge of the pool. "You're bending too much at the waist and then pulling your head up too soon."

"No offense," he said, totally intending to offend her. "But I feel like I could do it if I had a better teacher."

"You don't need a better teacher. You need to focus. I'm telling you what to do and you're doing the exact opposite."

"No, I need someone who isn't too afraid to get up here and show me."

She narrowed her eyes at him. "I'm not afraid."

"Prove it."

She stood and he had to force his gaze away from the top of her bathing suit, the clingy wet fabric showing the clear outline of her hardened nipples underneath. She brushed by him as she climbed the steps to the board and a shiver of excitement raced through him.

"Keep your arms over your head like this. Your fingers should hit the water before your head." She gave him several other instructions, but never actually left the board in demonstration. In fact, the longer she remained on the edge, the slower her voice became. "Jump high with your legs and d-di...di...dive—"

She shook her head as though to clear it. That's when he realized the rest of her body was trembling.

"Tessa?" Bypassing the rungs on the ladder, he jumped directly onto the board. "Are you okay?"

She stood at the edge, staring at the water. Her legs were locked together, her hands stiff at her sides. But still, she shook.

"I'm walking toward you," he said quietly, not wanting to spook her. "Give me your hand. I'll help you climb down."

"I d-don…don…" She paused and he had no doubt she was doing that thing where she closed her eyes any time she stuttered. "I don…don't want to climb down."

"Do you want me to stay up here with you?"

Tessa's nod was so slight, he thought he'd imagined it.

"I'm right here, behind you," he told her. "I'm not going anywhere."

This time, her nod was stronger. He could see her shoulder blades expand as she drew in a ragged breath. He realized that he'd been holding his own. "That's right. Just breathe."

They inhaled and exhaled together several times.

"I'm going to stand behind you, just in case…" He didn't want to say *panic attack*. The mere suggestion that she wasn't in control might send her into a tailspin. "Just in case you lose your balance."

She didn't object, so he moved closer and slowly

wrapped his right arm around her waist. "Here, lean back against me. I've got you."

Tessa's body was rigid, but at least her breathing remained controlled. After what seemed like several minutes, he felt her begin to relax against him. Her fingers rose to cover his hand, the one that was firmly planted above her belly button.

"I'm okay," she said, taking a few more deep breaths.

"You want to start backing up? I'll help you climb down."

"No," she said. "I need to get through this. I can do this if you're with me."

"I'm not going anywhere," he promised. Their skin was already dry and he worried that a chill would set in if they didn't either get out of these wet suits or back into the heated pool soon. "Tell me what we're working through."

"I need to dive." Her voice was still a little shaky, but determined.

"Okay, we'll dive together."

"No way." She managed a weak chuckle, but at least she was relaxing. "You're horrible at it."

"I was faking it," he admitted.

She rolled her eyes. "I know."

"So then why did you come up here to show me?"

"I needed to come up here for myself. I thought that if I had an audience, I could go through with it."

"You want to tell me what this is all about?" he tried again.

She sighed, then leaned her head back against his shoulder. "I used to be a diver. I was on the junior national team, training for the Olympics."

"I thought I'd read something in your case file about Olympic training, but I didn't know what sport."

She released a shuddering sigh of what sounded like relief. "Good to know my dad was able to keep some things covered up."

"What happened?"

"I had a bad accident my senior year of high school. It wasn't even during a meet or at practice or anything. Some of my teammates and I were messing around at the pool at Twin Kings. My mom had thrown one of her parties to celebrate us making the regional finals. 'Jump high and dive deep.' That's what my dad always told me."

Something clicked in Grayson's mind. Those same words had caused her to start stuttering earlier.

"But I was showing off. I went to do a backward arm-standing double somersault off our springboard. It's a dive that should only be done from a platform. I couldn't hold my position because the board dipped too low and when I overcorrected, my head hit the edge on my way down. I blacked out immediately and sank to the bottom of the pool. When I woke up from my coma, I was in the hospital. It was almost a week later."

Having experienced numerous hospitalizations with his sister, he knew exactly how terrifying that must've been for anyone, let alone someone so young. "That must've been scary."

The top of Tessa's head hit his chin as she nodded. "I couldn't see at first and thought I'd gone blind. And I couldn't talk, which was even scarier because I had so many questions. The surgeon explained that I had a TBI—traumatic brain injury. After a few days, my vision came back and I thought my speech would return just as easily. I could think of the words, but I couldn't make my tongue form them or my mouth say them. It was like there was a disconnect between my brain and my vocal chords. I spent almost two years in speech therapy relearning how to talk."

He knew the woman was tenacious, but he'd had no idea the obstacles she'd had to face to make it to the top of her profession. "And now you're on TV every night, talking in front of millions of people."

"That's the thing. My career depends on me not making any mistakes on the air. But suddenly I'm having panic attacks and stuttering, and everything that I've worked so hard to overcome is coming back full force."

"You're worried you're going to have a setback."

He brought his other arm around her waist, wishing he could use his body to comfort hers.

"In college, I tried to get back on the diving board and that's when I had my first panic attack. The fear was so intense that it caused me to regress, and set me back about six months in speech therapy. So when I had that panic attack at the funeral, I thought…"

"You thought it was happening again."

"Exactly. I let everyone think I was staying on at the ranch because of that whole Agent Steamy business. But that wasn't the scandal I was worried about. If I can't speak on the air, Grayson, my career is over."

He kissed her temple. "This isn't a relapse. I've seen you verbally spar with your family, and me, and anyone else who has tried to keep you from doing what you want to do. When you're confident and you believe in yourself, the words flow out of you and nobody dares to argue."

This time her chuckle was a little more natural. She'd made it through the worst part—admitting that she wasn't as strong as she pretended to be.

"So, what do we do?" Grayson asked, his lips still near her ear. "How can I help?"

Tessa exhaled loudly. "My dad always said we need to conquer our fears. Failure isn't an option."

"So, what's your fear?"

"Right now, it's jumping off this stupid diving board."

He laced his fingers through hers. "Hold my hand. I'll jump with you."

"That's even more dangerous. What if you crash into me?"

Grayson glanced down at the water. They were only a couple of feet above it and nowhere near the concrete edge. "You want to go first and I'll make sure you don't fall?"

"I don't know." He could feel her rib cage expand and contract under his hand.

"Then we'll just stay up here until you know."

"You're freezing, though," Tessa said.

"How do you know?"

"Because your nipples are so frozen, they're cutting into my back." Her shoulders wiggled against his chest.

"If you keep talking about my nipples," he whispered into her ear, "the rest of me will warm up a lot more quickly."

She laughed, but then her tone changed. "Okay, I'm going to do it." The resolve in her voice was clear.

"Warm me up? Or dive?"

"I'm going to jump off of here holding your hand. Feet first. Then, if I can do that, I'll try to dive. By myself."

As much as he wanted to keep Tessa in his arms,

he knew he had to help her get through this internal battle. "Okay. I'm going to squeeze in beside you. When you're ready, count us down."

She clutched his hand as he lowered his arm. Then, when they were side by side, he slipped his other hand into hers. He didn't say a word, even when they stood like that for at least thirty seconds. Grayson was beginning to think they'd both be going back down the ladder when she finally spoke.

Her voice was a little shaky, but she didn't stutter when she said, "Three... Two... One."

Silence pounded in Tessa's ears as she felt her body sink lower, her heart beating in her throat as she opened her eyes under the water. She blew out a stream of bubbles, noting that nothing had affected her vision this time. Grayson was beside her, although he'd released her hand and was holding up those silly piña colada shorts. She smiled to herself as she kicked her legs toward the surface.

"You did it!" Grayson used his free arm to dog-paddle to her.

"I did it," she repeated and wrapped her arms around his neck. The exhilaration racing through her body was so intense, she couldn't contain it. Tessa kissed him, but she was grinning too much to take things any further.

His smile must've equaled her own because she'd never seen Grayson look so happy. Who would have thought such a silly accomplishment of jumping feet-first off a diving board could inspire so much joy between two people who barely knew each other? Yet, seeing how proud he was sent a liberating shot of satisfaction through her. Tessa had a sudden urge to make him even prouder.

He spun her around triumphantly then asked, "Did it feel good?"

Their legs brushed against each other's as they kicked in place. "Not at first," she admitted. "It felt scary. But then it was over as soon as I jumped. It's more of a relief than anything."

"Do you want to try it again?" he asked.

She nodded and swam for the side railing to haul herself out. "You stay there. I'm going to jump to you."

She was like Marcus's twins when they'd been toddlers, wanting the thrill of the jump yet simul-taneously wanting the safety of someone catching them. The second time she went up on the diving board, she still paused for too long at the edge and felt the fear threatening to overrun her body.

"You've got this." Grayson held up his arms. "Jump toward me. I'll get you."

Tessa closed her eyes and leaped off with both sets of toes pointed perfectly down. She didn't sink as far this time and quickly resurfaced.

Grayson, true to his word, was less than an arm's length away from her. "You hardly made a splash."

The third time, she added a bounce before going straight in. The fourth time, she did a forward flip, not quite ready to go headfirst yet. Tessa did several more jumps, each time seeing Grayson's encouraging smile as soon as she resurfaced.

She lost count of how many times she went off the board but, finally, she was ready to try an actual dive. Tessa stopped halfway across the springboard. She took a deep breath and counted off how many steps she would need. One, two, three. Feet together, then bounce and lift. Her arms went up, her muscle memory overriding every anxiety. Without thinking about it, she pivoted midair, her head coming down and her legs straightening upward.

Not only did relief course through her, along with a tiny tremor of pride, Tessa experienced that tingling thrill that used to make her come alive when she was at a dive meet. She came from a family of overachievers. But diving was *her* specialty. It was her skill and made her stand out as her own person, not just another King. She hadn't realized she'd been chasing that same thrill, that same rush of accomplishment, since…well, since her last diving championship.

She heard one of the locker room doors creak open and turned her head in time to catch Grayson waving off Agent Talib. Tessa looked at the digital clock hanging next to the giant timer on the back wall.

Eleven twenty-seven. She blinked the chlorine out of her eyes to make sure she was reading the red numbers correctly.

"Why didn't you tell me how late it was getting?" she asked Grayson, who'd been treading water the entire time. He hadn't so much as swum to the edge for a break.

"Because I liked watching you." He kicked his way closer to her. His eyes were full of pride and perhaps something more. But it certainly wasn't exhaustion.

"We should probably get out," she suggested. Tessa's adrenaline levels were still too amped up to think about being tired, but she knew the exhaustion would set in soon enough. She swam to the ladder, but he didn't follow.

"You go ahead," he told her, a trace of pinkish color appearing on his cheeks. "I'll stay here for another minute or two."

"Why?" she asked before it dawned on her that he was using both arms to cut through the water to keep afloat. If he wasn't holding on to his shorts, then how were they...?

She looked toward the bright green, white and pink material crumpled in a heap at the bottom of the deep end. Her cheeks flooded with heat when she brought her eyes up to his. "Are you, um...?"

"Tessa?" He said her name as a warning and goose bumps spread along her wet skin. It reminded her of the way he'd warned her before that mind-searing kiss several nights ago.

"Yeah?" she asked, her voice raspy to her own ears. The only thing keeping her from seeing the man in all his naked glory was some lapping water. Awareness zipped through her, heightening her senses.

"There are two agents on the other side of that door."

"Right," she said, yanking her inappropriate thoughts back to reality. Ignoring the soreness in her muscles, she hauled herself out. Tessa had a feeling that if she wanted to, she could've tempted him into another kiss, or something more.

Unfortunately for her libido, though, she respected the man's principles too much to take advantage of him when he was naked in the pool.

As she grabbed her towel and headed for the women's locker room, she realized that by diving tonight, by overcoming one of her lingering fears, she was one step closer to returning to work. As soon as she left Wyoming, Grayson would officially be off assignment.

She would probably never see him again. Their lives were so different, there would never be a reason for their paths to cross.

But.

If she ever got the chance to pay him back for how

much he'd helped her tonight, Tessa hoped that she would be able to do so in person. And this time, she wouldn't let the rules get in the way.

Chapter Eleven

When Tessa informed the agents that she'd be returning to the community rec center the following evening, Grayson brought his own swimsuit. While she probably didn't need him in the pool with her again, he wanted to be ready just in case.

However, after Finn and Freckles arrived in the SUV behind them, there was no way he was about to get into the water with an audience there. Still, Grayson observed the situation from his self-designated position near the no-lifeguard-on-duty sign as she did a series of several dives, each one more complicated than the last. Each one also eliciting hearty whooping and clapping from her sister and aunt.

"Don't know why Sherilee was so nervous to come see this for herself." Freckles's voice was surprisingly quiet for once, although the acoustics made everything echo. "Tessa looks fantastic up there."

"Mom thought MJ was going to join a prison gang after spending one night in the Ridgecrest County drunk tank," Finn replied to her aunt. "When it comes to her kids, she's too much of a worrier and stresses out everyone else around her. It's better for all of our anxiety levels—especially Tessa's—if she doesn't come watch."

Grayson had no business voicing his agreement, but he did send up a silent word of thanks for small favors. Tessa might never return to her pre-Olympic-level diving form, but at least she was attempting the twists and flips with increasing boldness and determination. With her family there and her focus restored, she'd barely managed to glance in his direction, clearly no longer needing his emotional and physical support.

He clasped his hands behind his back uselessly. Tessa's renewed sense of confidence would motivate her to return to her job soon, which would allow him to return to his. Or, at least, his real job, rather than being a glorified watchdog. Plus, he really needed to look in on Maddie. While his mom kept him updated with the daily doctor reports, there was always that nagging worry in the back of his mind that both she and his sister were putting on a brave front just so he wouldn't stress about them.

There was a light at the end of this assignment tunnel, and Grayson waited for the calm sense of relief to settle over him the way it always did when he'd successfully accomplished a mission. Instead, an unexplained ball of loneliness formed in the pit of his stomach, growing each time Tessa jumped off that diving board.

The following night, Dahlia and Marcus both brought their kids to the community rec center to swim, turning the place into a King family pool party. Watching the twin boys chase each other across the slippery wet deck as Marcus argued with Violet in the shallow end made Grayson wish he'd brought a whistle.

By Friday night, Sherilee King must've overcome her own fears stemming from Tessa's accident because she arrived at the rec center pool with four more agents in tow, along with enough pizzas to feed half the county. The woman could barely stay in one place because she was too busy pacing and wringing her hands every time Tessa was up on the high dive. Whenever her daughter resurfaced, though, Mrs. King's face lit up with both relief and pride.

"You gotta eat, Agent Wyatt." Aunt Freckles passed him a paper plate filled with two slices of deep dish loaded with melted cheese and nearly every topping offered at the Pepperoni Stampede, the local pizza parlor in the small town of Teton Ridge.

"Thanks," he said, accepting the plate and letting

the scent of garlic and spicy sausage remind him that he'd only had a protein bar for lunch.

"I should be the one thanking you," the older woman said, tilting her peach-colored tower of curls at Tessa up on the diving board. "You're the one who got our girl back on her horse, so to speak."

He ignored the tingle of pride pulling his shoulders back and bit into the first slice. If he kept his mouth full, she wouldn't expect him to respond. Grayson knew when someone was fishing for information, especially when that someone was the least subtle person he'd ever met. Still, he wasn't about to discuss Tessa's TBI or her fear of having another panic attack, even if it was with her well-meaning aunt.

But Aunt Freckles was like a dog with a bone. "SAIC Simon told us there'd be a family debriefing tomorrow morning. I'm assuming that can only mean that you're all pulling up stakes and heading back to Washington."

Actually, Grayson had put in a request for a few days' leave so he could travel to Maryland first to check in on Maddie and his mom. He hadn't put in his official transfer request yet, but was hoping to once they cleared out of Twin Kings. Luckily, he was saved from answering.

"You're not even offering anyone the Garden Party pizza, Freckles." Mrs. King took the plate holding Grayson's remaining slice from his hand

and swapped it out for a one containing a triangular shape of mixed veggies held together by a layer of underseasoned, edible cardboard. "Too much lactose and processed meat will just clog you up and slow you down, Agent. Plant-based foods are the way to go. You'll thank me later."

"Sherilee, you can't just steal a man's food like that," Freckles chided.

When Mrs. King showed no sign of returning the swapped-out paper plate to Grayson anytime soon, Freckles used her brightly manicured fingers to snatch his stolen slice of supreme pizza back from her sister-in-law and dropped it directly onto his plate. Now he had a total of three pieces of pizza— or at least two and a half since he still had his original slice in his right hand.

Despite the past three weeks, these women were still in the throes of an absurd power struggle, and their family and half of the agents were smart enough to stay well clear of them. Grayson had no desire to be one of the pawns in this pizza saga and took a discreet step backward, his exit strategy already in place.

"Hold on a second, Agent Grayson Wyatt!" Mrs. King reached for his elbow.

"You don't have to be so damn formal all the time, Sherilee." Freckles rolled her eyes so dramatically, he worried that one of her false eyelashes would stick to her penciled eyebrow. "Just call him Agent Wyatt.

Or better yet, Grayson. He's practically part of the family by now."

Whoa. A shiver of discomfort zipped down Grayson's spine. He didn't *want* to be considered part of the family and squared his shoulders as professionally as possible before addressing Mrs. King. "Agent Wyatt is fine, ma'am."

"I apologize for my sister-in-law, Agent Wyatt. I think all that aerosol hairspray has gone to her head." Mrs. King made a tsking sound. "She isn't very good with boundaries."

"Gimme a break, Sherilee." Freckles stage-whispered out of the corner of her heavily painted lips, "I apologize for *my* sister-in-law, Agent Wyatt. She never wants anyone to know she grew up in a run-down trailer park in Laramie, so she tends to overcompensate with the whole 'lady of the manor' act."

"An act?" Mrs. King snorted a very unladylike snort. "That's rich coming from a woman who'd rather serve hash browns and unwanted opinions than use her famous surname to actually help her community. Because heaven forbid anyone associate you with that founding family whose name appears on various hospital wings, Ivy League campuses and the Declaration of Independence."

Wait. Grayson's eyes flew back and forth between the two older women. He'd once seen Freckles listed in Rider King's file, but he'd simply thought she was just some café owner from Idaho. He hadn't put two and two together and realized she was part of *that* family.

Before Grayson could ask, Freckles waved a hand in the air—the rows of colorful plastic-beaded bracelets on her wrist clinking together—and asked, "Are we gonna stand here arguing about our dead ancestors or are we gonna show Agent Wyatt our appreciation for helping Tessa get her head on straight?"

Neither, Grayson prayed.

"I'm just glad you're admitting that something other than your high-calorie comfort food you 'prescribed—'" Mrs. King's jeweled fingers made air quotes at the last words "—is what helped Tessa."

"Maybe if you ate something sweet once in a while, you wouldn't be such a..." Freckles continued the argument as Grayson turned all of his focus to finishing his pizza.

Outside, it was nearly thirty degrees and the forecast was calling for the first snowstorm of the new year. Maybe Grayson could offer Doherty a case of beer and tickets to the Red Sox home opener if he'd switch posts right this second. Nah. Every other agent on duty would rather be knee-deep in a blizzard than be trapped in a steamy, chlorinated room with these two battling sister-in-laws.

Grayson scanned the indoor pool, hoping one of the King siblings would come to his rescue. Unfortunately, the cavalry had been dealing with these women way longer than he had. That meant they knew better than to get caught in the cross fire.

As the petty insults flew back and forth, Grayson's mind zeroed in on a sudden realization. None of these King women fit the mold of what society expected. Sherilee King was the overly dignified one, yet grew up in a trailer park. Freckles actually came from an even more famous family with obscene amounts of wealth and privilege. Dahlia had a degree in interior design but owned a former brothel. Finn could've been mistaken for a college cheerleader yet single-handedly ran one of the biggest cattle operations in the state of Wyoming. And then there was Tessa...

Grayson was barely skimming the surface on the hidden depths Tessa kept well guarded. Nothing in the prebriefing files and intelligence reports had prepared him for any of this. This whole family had gone from code names on a chart to very real people with very real backgrounds and personalities. And if he stayed around much longer, the very realness of Tessa would make it that much more difficult for him to file everything away and forget it after the final post-op briefing.

"So, Agent Wyatt?" Mrs. King waved her palm in front of his face and Grayson snapped to attention. "I was hoping you'd have a moment before the briefing tomorrow morning to meet with Sonya."

He shook his head to clear it. "Who's Sonya?"

"She's the head of my public relations team."

Grayson twisted his empty paper plate in his hands. He was familiar with the army of assistants and press secretaries on the former second lady's staff. None of them was named Sonya.

Freckles must have sensed his confusion because she clarified, "Sherilee hired Sonya to help with Mitchell Junior's situation."

Grayson remained motionless. "But that assignment falls under Echo Team. Don't you want to meet with Agent Franks?" Franks had been assigned to MJ the night of his arrest, and had later been assigned to tail him to and from court for his arraignment, as well as around the ranch after he'd made bail.

"Of course. There's just one pesky little issue we need to wrap up."

"What issue is that?" Grayson's lips pressed flat.

"My son Marcus informed me there's a video of Tessa exchanging words with you in the staging center outside my husband's funeral. Apparently, Congressman Davis's assistant has made several inquiries about the footage."

A chill went down Grayson's spine. He immediately knew what this was about.

"I was there." Freckles jerked a thumb at her chest. "Trust me, there wasn't much exchanging on Agent Wyatt's end. Just Tessa cussing up a blue streak and giving him holy hell for taking her for a ride in her daddy's hearse."

"Could you please not make it sound so crude?" Mrs. King's forced smile looked more like a grimace. "Anyway, I'm concerned that the video might not show my daughter in the most favorable light."

It really didn't show either Tessa *or* Grayson in a favorable light. Especially because Grayson was the one being accused of not following proper protocol and might possibly have to answer to his superiors at an inquiry board.

Grayson's stance widened as he prepared to defend himself against a still unknown threat. "Ma'am, it's my understanding that the video was obtained from the body cam of one of the Ridgecrest County deputy sheriffs. As long as nobody tampered with the footage, it's an accurate portrayal of the events as they happened."

"I understand how the recording was acquired, Agent. My concern is the reason why the congressman is so interested in accessing it."

"Well…" He tilted his head, knowing no other way to put this delicately. "The video is a matter of public record. I don't see how the sheriff could keep it from him."

"Oh, public records go missing all the time," Mrs. King replied, and Grayson really hoped she wasn't about to suggest something illegal. "But not in Teton Ridge and not while my son is in charge. Hell, Marcus put his own brother in jail. There's no way he'd 'accidentally misplace—'" she used the finger quotes again "—the video just to protect Tessa's reputation. So, while I might not be able to get rid of it myself, there's always a way to spin things to one's advantage. After all, I haven't gotten to where I am today without being proactive."

A muscle spasmed in his clenched jaw as Grayson easily guessed Mrs. King's so-called proactive route. There was no way she'd spin anything to *his* advantage. But before he could ask her for clarification, Rider King yelled across the pool.

"Hey, Sherilee, I told you I hadn't lost my favorite bathing suit!" The old man waved the bright piña colada–printed shorts over his head like a battle flag as he walked toward them. "Although, I have no idea how they ended up in the lost and found basket at the rec center."

"You sure did," Mrs. King told her brother-in-law, but her smile didn't quite reach her eyes.

"Hey, wifey." Rider wiggled his bushy gray eyebrows at Freckles. "I'm gonna throw these things on real quick and then I'll meet you in the hot tub."

"Stop calling me *wifey*, you crazy old man," Freckles shot back. Then she winked at Grayson before following her ex-husband to the men's locker room.

"I told Mitchell Junior to get rid of that tacky bathing suit years ago," Mrs. King told Grayson as she waved at one of her grandsons who'd just executed a perfect cannonball. Then she lowered her voice. "Let this be a lesson to you, Agent Wyatt. Nothing ever stays hidden unless you hide it yourself."

The woman soon found another agent in need of her plant-based Garden Party pizza, but Grayson wasn't quite ready to breathe a sigh of relief just yet. There was no doubt in his mind that Sherilee King intended on saving her daughter's reputation by throwing him under the bus. He had no idea how she'd do it, but she clearly thought he was foolish enough to be an active participant in her plan.

And for what?

Was his career really worth Tessa suffering a little bit of negative press? She worked in the media, herself. It was her own colleagues who'd gotten her into this situation in the first place. Being at the Twin Kings Ranch these past few weeks almost made him forget how much he hated all these powerful people with their mind games and their publicity stunts. Almost.

Grayson didn't think his jaw could get any more rigid, but it did. He just needed to get through one more day. Then he could close the file on this family for good.

Tessa hadn't been able to get Grayson alone since that first night at the pool when he'd convinced her to go off that diving board. Something had clicked in her brain that evening, and each night that she'd gone to the pool, she grew more and more convinced that she was ready to return to work.

Sure, she might have another panic attack at some point down the road. Nothing was ever certain when it came to traumatic brain injuries. Yet, Tessa was now armed with the confidence that she could face the fear and work through it.

She was done with hiding out and being shielded from the world's reaction to an injury she might never overcome. In fact, she'd spoken to her boss yesterday and planned to be back in the studio by Monday evening. That meant today would be her last day at Twin Kings.

Tessa stepped out of the shower and saw a text alert on her smartphone. Her mom had sent today's agenda to all the siblings. There was a family briefing planned for eleven o'clock and a conference call planned with some PR expert named Sonya at one. Tessa still didn't see a need for the public relations team just yet. What she did see a need for, though, was talking to Grayson one-on-one.

The digital clock on her phone read 10:08 a.m. and she tapped at the screen with her thumb before realizing she didn't even have his number in her list of contacts. Her legs grew restless and she couldn't get dressed quickly enough.

Her last relationship, as well as the one before that, had been conducted mostly through texts and emails and video chats. Yet all her interactions with

Grayson had been in person. It was a weird feeling to realize that in less than twelve hours, she wouldn't be able to simply walk outside and have him magically appear. She wouldn't have any way of getting in touch with him after today.

Maybe it was for the best.

Sure, she'd kissed the man and shared some of her most personal secrets with him. However, as much as they'd talked about something physical happening between them when his assignment was officially over, was she truly ready to go there? Once she returned to her own life, all of these feelings that had been building inside her would likely run out of steam without him there to fuel the fire.

Still. She needed to at least say goodbye to him without an audience. Tessa couldn't afford to leave any loose strings untied—she'd learned her lesson after Davis—and they both deserved the closure. Plus, she wanted Grayson to know that he'd been an instrumental part in her getting through the past three weeks.

Leaving the main house, Tessa kept close to the line of trees that ran the length of the road between the stables and the bunkhouse. Did her attempts to be discreet really matter, though? Everyone on this ranch was always watching. Hell, she'd been shadowed almost half of her life by either bodyguards or Secret Service agents or paparazzi. She strode into the middle of the path to walk the rest of the way. There was no sense in sneaking around now.

She lifted her hand to knock on the bunkhouse door, not wanting to barge into the agents' private retreat, the only place on these fifty-five-thousand-plus acres where they could get away from the members of the King family.

Doherty, the agent who always wore a friendly smile and a Boston Red Sox cap, opened the door. "Hey, Precis— I mean, Miss King. The briefing isn't here. It's in the conference room next door."

"I know." She swallowed down her embarrassment and straightened her shoulders. The trick was to act as though it was perfectly natural for her to show up at the bunkhouse unannounced. To act as though *they* should've been expecting *her*. She wasn't Sherilee King's daughter for nothing. "I'm looking for Agent Wyatt."

"Right," Doherty said, stepping aside. "I think I saw him in the kitchen. Make yourself at home."

The agent left and Tessa let herself into the bunkhouse, which appeared to be empty. The beds were neatly made and several stuffed duffel bags sat on the floor at the end of the bunks, as though the inhabitants had already packed for a quick departure. Tessa's stomach sank when she was presented with the evidence of how eager everyone was to leave Twin Kings.

Prior to today, she'd never needed to enter this

particular building on the ranch and now she had to take a guess as to which side housed the restroom and which side housed the kitchen. She made her way through the open floor plan until she came to the alcove that held a large dining table.

She was at the swinging door that must've separated the kitchen from the living quarters when she heard Grayson's voice. "Is the doctor concerned about the rod?"

"No," a woman's voice responded, sounding a bit echoey and delayed. "They said it sometimes takes longer to fuse, depending on the patient. Maddie is older than most of the people she's operated on, so her bones are already fully developed. We knew going in that it might take longer."

That must be Grayson's mother on a video conference call. Tessa should turn around and leave, but her feet wouldn't budge. She'd been researching EDMD since Grayson had first told her about his sister, and her curiosity wouldn't simply vanish just because it was the polite thing to do. Or because HIPAA regulations required it.

"I knew we shouldn't have waited so long," Grayson said, his voice tense. "She should've had the procedure done years ago."

"Stop beating yourself up, Gray," the woman replied, then made a yawning sound. "You can't work thirty hours of overtime in a day that only has twenty-four hours in it. If it weren't for you, Maddie wouldn't have even been able to have the surgery in the first place. Let alone any of the other treatments you pay for."

"I just hate it that you both are going through this and I'm not there to help, Mom."

Tessa could imagine the stiffness of his jaw. It was how he always looked whenever he wanted to fix something or when something was holding him back.

Oh no.

A wave of realization smacked into Tessa, and her hand flew to her mouth.

She was currently the "something" holding Grayson back from being with his family. She'd been selfishly hiding away on the ranch, licking her wounds and trying to overcome the aftereffects of her TBI, while all of the agents assigned to babysit her—especially Grayson—needed to return to their real lives.

"I know you're not allowed to give us details about your assignment, Grayson, but Maddie said she thinks it should be over soon. You'll come and see us afterward, right?" His mom's voice held a trace of optimism despite all the setbacks life had seemed to throw her family's way.

"As soon as I get the green light, I'll be on a plane to Baltimore," Grayson promised, and Tessa cringed knowing that the supposed green light would come as soon as she was out of his life. "Is now a good time to talk to Maddie?"

There was a pause on the other side of the door and then some mumbling from his mom, who was maybe talking to a nurse or someone else in the hospital room. Tessa was already gripped by so much guilt for being the cause of Grayson missing out on time with his sister, she didn't need to add eavesdropping to the list.

She glanced at the clock on the wall as she debated whether to leave. The briefing started in ten minutes and she wouldn't get a chance to talk to Grayson alone if she didn't wait for him here. She was about to turn from the door and linger by the entrance to the bunkhouse when his little sister's words stopped her.

"Hey there, Agent Steamy. How's the beautiful and talented Miss King?"

"You know that I'm not at liberty to say, Mads. But if you want to ask her yourself, you can."

Grayson swung through the door right then, holding an open laptop in front of him. Tessa's cheeks flooded with heat, her eyelids stretching into wide circles. Of course he'd known that she'd been there, on the other side of the door. The man had a sixth sense when it came to her, always appearing when she wasn't expecting it.

Tessa held up her palms, madly waving them back and forth as her eyes implored him not to turn that laptop around. He tilted his head and lifted the corner of his mouth. The knowing dare coming from his eyes suggested that if she didn't want to be a part of the conversation, then she should've walked away instead of listening in.

Grayson swung the laptop screen around, and Tessa summoned every ounce of professional stage training she possessed to fix her expression from one of mortification to one of pleasant surprise. "Hi! You must be Maddie."

"Oh my gosh!" The young woman blinked several times. "It really is you. Mom, it's really her."

"Hello, Miss King!" Mrs. Wyatt's face appeared on the screen as she squeezed in next to her daughter's hospital bed. "I'm a big fan. I watch your show whenever I get the chance. It's a pleasure to meet you."

"It's a pleasure to meet both of you, as well. Grayson has told me so much about you." Tessa realized her mistake as soon as she saw the smaller woman use her elbow to nudge her mother.

"Grayson?" Maddie squinted at the camera. "My brother, Grayson, talked to you? About us?"

Tessa chuckled, relieved his tendency to be tight-lipped wasn't because of her. "Well, it was like pulling teeth to get him to talk, but we've had a lot of downtime up here on the ra—"

"Our location is classified information." Grayson slapped his hand over the speaker, and in doing so, brought himself next to Tessa so that they were now side by side, facing the laptop.

Maddie rolled her eyes. "I'm pretty sure everyone who has access to a TV or the internet knows where Tessa King has been hiding out these past couple of weeks."

This time, it was Mrs. Wyatt using her elbow to gently nudge her daughter. "What Maddie meant to say is that we watched your father's funeral and, like the rest of the world, we're very sorry for your recent loss."

"Thank you." Tessa replied to the condolences somewhat robotically because she was still stuck on the two words causing her guilt to resurface. *Hiding out.* She was the reason this young woman didn't have her brother by her side in the hospital. Clearing her throat, she changed the subject. "So, Maddie, how are you feeling? Grayson told me you had surgery recently."

Should Tessa have mentioned the surgery? Maybe Maddie Wyatt didn't want some stranger knowing her personal business. Tessa tried not to cast a questioning glance at Grayson as she waited for the other woman to respond. Luckily, she didn't have to wait long.

"Well, the recovery is taking way longer than I was hoping. I went home last week, but then I got super sick and my surgeon was worried about infection, so they readmitted me to the hospital and put me on this mega antibiotic. I'm feeling better now, so it looks like the doc will let me start physical therapy soon. If the procedure works and the rod fuses to my spine, I'm hoping to get back in the pool soon. Maybe even go for a ride on one of the horses at this equestrian center out in the country. Have you guys been doing any riding?"

"*I've* been riding. Your brother has been…" Tessa tapped a finger to her lips. "Well, I don't know what to call his technique on the back of a horse."

When Maddie grinned, even on the screen, Tessa could feel the joy radiating off her. "It's called clinging to the saddle for dear life as he yells at everyone to slow down."

"I'm not that bad." Grayson smiled at his sister and Tessa's heart turned into a puddle.

"Man, I wish I was up there with you guys in Wyoming," Maddic said. "I'd love to see all your horses."

"Perhaps when you're feeling better, we can…" Tessa trailed off as Grayson's elbow lightly pressed into her upper arm, a warning of some sort. Perhaps there was something about his sister's prognosis he hadn't wanted to share.

"Listen, Mads. We have a briefing meeting in about three minutes," Grayson said, immediately filling the silence. "We have to go. I'll call you tomorrow."

"Fine," Maddie replied. "It was nice to meet you, Miss King, even if my brother won't let you make any promises to me about visiting when I feel better. Love you, Gray."

The young woman was extremely astute. An invitation to come riding on the ranch was exactly what Tessa had been about to offer. And she had a feeling that was exactly why Grayson had cut her off.

"Love you, too, Mads. Give Mom a kiss for me," Grayson added at the last second, but the screen had already gone dark.

With the call disconnected, an awkward silence hung between them. Tessa rocked back on her heels, debating whether she could pretend that she'd stumbled into the bunkhouse instead of the conference room by mistake.

"So—" he tucked the closed laptop under his arm and turned to face her "—were you looking for me?"

They were alone amid the rows of beds. After she'd been caught eavesdropping on his private conversation. There was no denying her breach into his personal space. Tessa took a deep breath and came clean. "Yeah, I was hoping to talk to you before the briefing."

"Is it to tell me that you're going back to DC tonight?" he asked, his face perfectly devoid of expression one way or another. "Your network is already running an ad promoting your return on Monday night."

Tessa knew he didn't think very highly of her job, which was part of the reason she was eager to return to it. She needed to put some distance between them before things went too far.

She needed to make sure that her attraction to him wasn't based on the fact that he'd protected her time and again. That he'd been the one to rescue her, even from her own fears. For all she knew, she could simply be suffering from some sort of damsel-in-distress syndrome. Hooking up with the bodyguard was such a cliché, and Tessa was much too analytical for something like that. If she was going to have sex with a man, she had to be sure it was for the right reasons. And she couldn't be sure of that until she was back to being on her own.

"I'm flying out tonight. But before I left, I wanted to thank you for…" *Don't say* rescue, she warned herself. It would only remind them both of how much she'd needed saving and skew the already uneven power balance between them. At the same time, she truly was grateful to him. "I wanted to thank you for everything. I know that you gave up so much in your personal life to stay on longer at the ranch. I also know you had to deal with a lot of teasing with that whole Agent Steamy thing."

"That's part of the job description," he replied, and her chest sank from the hollowness of his words. At least he hadn't said that he'd been paid for putting up with her. That would've been more insulting than anything.

Closure, she reminded herself. *Tie those loose*

strings. She inhaled and continued. "Anyway, I know we talked about what would happen between, uh, us when you were officially off duty. But I don't want you thinking that I'm going to hold you to that."

"Don't worry." His eyes turned to a stormy gray as he crossed his arms in front of his chest. "I copy you loud and clear."

Reaching out, she placed her palm on his forearm and felt his muscles flinch underneath. Great, now she'd insulted him. She dropped her hand. "I'm not saying that the attraction is no longer there. I just need to be smarter about how I act upon it."

Grayson's eyes scanned the room, always on the alert. "Perhaps the smart thing to do would be for you not to act on that attraction at all."

"Possibly," she admitted, realizing that maybe his own attraction was waning now that he no longer had to swoop in and play the hero. "The thing is, not only am I still grieving, I also just came out of a very public breakup. Even though it was a long time coming, if people think I jumped from one relationship to another, they'll be questioning my emotional state."

"We certainly can't have that." He stared at his watch, as though he was already bored with the conversation. "Is there a public relations person for ending things with the bodyguard, as well? Because I don't know if I can take another meeting with your mother and Sonya What's-Her-Name, no matter how hot the kisses are between us."

Tessa's brows slammed together, but before she could respond, there was a loud knock outside the bunkhouse. Agent Doherty cracked the door and yelled inside, "Briefing starts next door in thirty seconds."

She couldn't promise that their attraction would last once they left Wyoming. Even if it did, she couldn't promise that any sort of physical relationship would be worth the price they'd both have to pay publicly. So Tessa held her tongue as she followed him to the conference room.

Luckily, she didn't have to promise him anything. Her flight left before she got the chance to see Grayson again.

Chapter Twelve

Grayson flew back to Washington, DC, for a formal debriefing with his entire unit. As SAIC Simon had predicted, the internal affairs department wanted to review the incident at Roper King's funeral, the one that had led to Grayson meeting Tessa.

He had to sit through several interviews and at least two screenings of the video of Tessa lambasting him over his procedure. The inquiry board informed him they'd let him know the results of their investigation when it was completed. Of course, there was no time frame for how long that might take, but Grayson took solace in the fact that he was being allowed to operate with Delta Team's protective detail while he awaited their decision.

Grayson enjoyed two days' leave with Maddie and his mom before being called back for another assignment. This time, his team was traveling to Philadelphia to protect a group of foreign heads of state sightseeing the birthplace of Independence.

The dignitaries and their aides had their own security teams and all were staying on the top floor of the Ritz-Carlton. The Secret Service agents were a secondary line of defense and their RON—remain overnight—status meant they were doubling up in rooms on the floor below. Grayson had drawn the short straw and been paired with Doherty, but luckily they were working opposite shifts and he didn't have to put up with the man's snoring. Or his wisecracking.

Until the night Doherty returned to the room unexpectedly to dress in his undercover clothes.

"Change of venues tonight," Doherty said as he stopped at the hallway closet to hang up his suit jacket. "The prime minister's daughter talked her old man into taking her to a Sixers' game. If I show up to the arena wearing a button-up shirt and tie, someone might mistake me for one of the coaches."

Grayson squinted at Doherty's five-foot-seven-inch frame. "I'm pretty sure nobody's going to mistake you for a basketball coach."

Grayson lounged on top of the bed, still fully dressed from his earlier shift, waiting for his roommate to finish changing in the bathroom so that he could take a shower. He turned on the television set and half-heartedly began flipping through the channels.

Grayson froze when he landed on Tessa King's perfectly polished image on the screen. Her hair was in a tight bun and her makeup was thicker than it had been on the ranch. In fact, she almost resembled a totally different woman than the one he'd spent time with on Twin Kings. He was so focused on analyzing her controlled posture and the way she kept eye contact with the camera that he didn't even hear what she was saying.

Unfortunately, he also didn't hear Doherty exit the bathroom. "You gonna go out tonight or are you just gonna stay in and make cow eyes over your girl, there?"

"No." Grayson cleared his throat. "I was actually looking for a local news station, but all the channels on these hotel TVs are never the same. And she's not 'my girl.'"

He aimed the remote control at the screen, but instead of turning it off, he turned up the volume. Tessa's voice was strong and precise, and sent a wave of awareness through his bloodstream.

"Right." Doherty slid his holstered duty weapon onto his old leather belt. "Have you talked to her since Wyoming?"

"No." Grayson managed to keep his voice neutral while he fumbled with the remote again until he found the mute button. It wasn't like Tessa had slipped him her phone number or told him to stay in touch before she'd gone wheels up.

"Uh-huh. So then you probably don't know that she's here in Philadelphia right now?"

Grayson's head snapped up. He looked between Doherty and the television that showed her talking, even though he could no longer hear what she was saying.

"It's not a live broadcast, Agent Steamy." Doherty retrieved his Red Sox cap from the top of the dresser. "That episode was prerecorded."

"How do you know she's in Philly?"

"Because I'm a Secret Service agent and it's my job to know things." Doherty straightened his earpiece as he crossed the room to the door. "Plus, I saw her name on the reservation desk's computer when I ran the guest list against our security threat database."

Grayson's muscles tightened. "You mean she's staying here at this hotel?"

"If you're asking out of a personal interest, then I can neither confirm nor deny that. But if you're only interested because you feel a certain professional courtesy toward her—say for example you wanted to advise her that the ice machine on her floor was out of order—then I'd tell you she's in room seven nineteen." Doherty chuckled knowingly as he walked out the door.

Grayson jumped to his feet and paced the room, trying not to glance at the hotel telephone on the desk. It had been over three weeks since he'd last seen Tessa. He didn't dare show up at her room. For all he knew, she could be in town to meet some guy. Grayson wasn't about to knock on her door only to be greeted by her date. His fingers dug into his palm before his brain reminded him that Tessa King was no longer his concern.

Although—he allowed his eyes to land on the phone—she'd probably appreciate him calling her to warn her that he was there, as well. Just in case they ran into each other in the lobby or something. He wouldn't want things to be awkward between them if he caught her by surprise.

Before he could talk himself out of it, he had the receiver in his hand and punched in seven-one-nine on the number pad.

It rang twice before she answered. "Hello?"

Grayson's heart thumped behind his rib cage. "Miss King?"

"Who is this?" she asked without confirming her identity. Clearly, this wasn't the first time someone unexpected had gotten access to her room number.

"It's Agent Wyatt."

He heard the catch in her breath. "Grayson?"

So much for keeping things from turning personal. And, really, there was no longer any reason why they needed to maintain that professional

boundary. He scrubbed a hand over his jaw and decided to leap clear across that once blurry line.

"Do you want to go get a drink?"

Grayson half expected her to show up in the bright
red tailored suit and sleeked-back hair she'd been
wearing when she'd been on his TV earlier.

So, an hour later, when Tessa walked into the
nearly empty neighborhood bar down the street
from their hotel wearing jeans, riding boots and a
soft green knit cap over her loose blond curls, his
heart beat faster. Now, *this* was the relaxed version
of Tessa, the one he'd spent so much time with on
the ranch.

"Hey," he said, rising from his seat.

He'd hoped the place would have some discreet
booths tucked in the back where they could talk privately. Unfortunately, when he'd arrived, his choices
had been several vacant stools lining one corner of
the massive black-lacquered bar or a handful of tall
tables stationed directly in front of the plate-glass
windows. Knowing that it could seriously affect their
careers if the press caught wind of them being there
together, Grayson had chosen the corner where she
wouldn't be on display to anyone passing by outside.
Not that many people were out for a casual stroll this
late on a blustery February weeknight.

She must've read his mind because she immediately scanned the room as though looking for anyone

who might recognize her. It was nearly ten o'clock on a Tuesday night, so the place was empty except for the bartender and a guy in a bright green Eagles hoodie who only seemed interested in the car restoration show on the TV behind the bar.

Tessa shrugged out of her suede coat and asked, "How'd you find this place?"

"Doherty recommended it. He makes it a priority to know all of the less conspicuous drinking establishments within a fifteen-mile radius of wherever we're stationed."

She pulled off her knit cap and set it on the shiny bar top before running a hand through her hair. Grayson's fingers twitched at the memory of touching the same silky strands over a month ago. Thirty-eight days. Not that he was keeping count.

"So Agent Doherty knows we're here?"

Grayson wasn't about to mention that Doherty was the one who'd casually suggested he contact her. "Let's just say he's a wealth of information when it comes to tactical planning and logistics."

The bartender took a break from folding white dishrags and asked for their order. The woman was older, with a stocky build and a disinterested expression. She reminded him of Gunnery Sergeant Haggerty, his senior drill instructor who'd seen everything but, because he'd been closing in on retirement, hadn't wanted to write up any reports.

If the bartender recognized Tessa King, she didn't

let on. Grayson passed the woman a twenty-dollar bill and murmured, "Thanks," after she handed them their drinks.

He nodded at Tessa's plain-looking vodka and soda before picking up his own pilsner. "No beer for you tonight?"

"Nope." She took a careful sip. "It goes down too easily and I wanted to make sure I have a clear head."

Dread crawled through his chest as he waited for her to politely tell him that what had happened between them on the ranch was a one-off. That their fleeting attraction had been the result of forced proximity. But she didn't say anything else.

The guy at the other end of the bar paid his tab and left. The bartender asked if they needed anything before she stepped out back for a smoke. And still, he and Tessa sat there quietly as though neither one of them knew what to say to the other. Maybe having those boundaries of him being on assignment had actually made them both feel safer. Like they could dip their toes in the water, but always had a built-in excuse for why they couldn't fully immerse themselves.

"Are you in Philadelphia for work?" he finally asked, wondering if things were this awkward between Freckles and Rider King when they'd seen each other again. Probably not.

Tessa nodded. "I'm following a lead on a story about election fraud in the next county over. Investigative journalism isn't really my thing, but the whistleblower claimed he'd only talk to me. According to my producer, all that media coverage following my dad's funeral put me in a more sympathetic light and made me seem more approachable."

He finished his icy beer quickly, washing down the memory of Davis Townsend telling Tessa she was a cold, cutthroat bitch. When Grayson had intervened, he'd been hoping the congressman would resist the directive to walk out of the stables, thereby requiring a forced escort.

He flexed his fingers after he set down his empty glass. "I'm glad things are working out for you. Careerwise."

"How about you?" She pivoted slightly on her bar stool. "What brings you to Philadelphia?"

He explained that he was on a protective detail with some foreign dignitaries, but didn't give any specifics.

"So you're back on the job." Tessa studied him. "I'm glad all that business in Wyoming didn't get you into any hot water with your bosses."

"Well, the inquiry board is still investigating." It helped that none of the Kings had filed a formal complaint. "So they haven't taken my badge yet."

"Speaking of your badge…" She took another sip of her drink before moving in closer. Her knee glazed against his and his pulse skyrocketed. "You told me there would come a time when you were no longer on duty."

There was no mistaking the intent in her eyes. It had been the exact same look she'd given him on Pine Top Point. Just like then, his desire threatened to consume him. Unlike then, though, he no longer had to fight to control it. Anticipation raced through him as he flashed a wide grin.

"I am definitely off duty. At least, where you're concerned." He placed his hands on either side of her face and pulled her mouth against his. He stroked his tongue against her lips and when she opened up to him, he kissed her slowly and thoroughly—not caring about his promise to her that the next time they got physical, she could be in the driver's seat.

Later on, they'd have all the time in the world to take turns being in control.

"Grayson?" She pulled back, her lips already swollen and her eyelids half-closed. "Take me back to the hotel."

Tessa's pulse pounded in her ears as she rode the elevator alone to her room. Although Grayson was technically off his shift, he explained that he still had to keep a low profile while inside the hotel and would follow her using the service elevator.

It was for the best, she reminded herself as her fingers drummed against the brass handrail. Neither one of them wanted to risk being seen together in the lobby. Scratch that, Tessa thought as the number for her floor lit up and the doors opened. Being seen in public with Grayson wouldn't be the worst thing in the world. For her, at least. She hadn't been lying when she'd told Grayson that the public's perception of her had changed after the pictures of them together had surfaced.

Tessa let herself into her room and barely had enough time to shrug out of her coat before there was a discreet knock on the door. Grayson stood in the hallway in his jeans and a snug black T-shirt under an open shearling-lined coat, his gaze just as intense as it had been at the bar. All the blood rushed to her head and she braced her hand on the doorjamb to steady herself. *This is really happening.*

"Are you okay?" he asked, concern immediately replacing the passion in his expression.

"Grayson..." She moved to the side, refusing to let her knees buckle as she held the door open for him. "I'm no longer the damsel in distress. You don't have to treat me with kid gloves."

"Good." He dipped his head as he passed through the open door, dragging his eyes down the length of her and then back up. As though he was calculating which part of her body he wanted to caress first. "Because the wait nearly killed me."

The next thing she knew, the door whooshed closed with a definite click and her shoulder blades were arching into the entryway wall. Her arms circled his neck and his hands followed the outline of her curves until settling under her rear end. He barely had to apply any upward pressure and she was lifting her legs, wrapping them around his waist as he thrust his tongue deeper into her mouth.

He groaned and pressed closer. Using his body to brace Tessa against the wall, he peeled his hands away from her butt long enough to shrug out of his jacket. She took the opportunity to tug on the soft cotton fabric between his shoulder blades and pulled the T-shirt over his head.

The motion broke their kiss, but it also allowed him to return the favor. Grayson made quick work of her sweater and the camisole underneath. She leaned forward so that he could access her bra clasp and he secured her hips under one forearm as he set her aching breasts free.

He kissed her again, their bare chests coming together. She moaned as tingling sensations shot through her tightly budded nipples. Recklessness coursed through her and she slid her hands over the smooth, warm ridges of his biceps, pulling him in even tighter so that she could fuse the heat of her skin with his.

Tessa had always been so precise, so careful, so controlled. She needed to let go and Grayson was only too willing to oblige her. She nipped at his lower lip and said, "Take me to the bed."

"Not yet," he murmured against her lips. "Next

time, we'll make it to the bed. But right now, I need you here."

He elevated her even higher and spun them toward the entryway table. When he swung her onto the edge, something went crashing to the floor. Maybe it was a lamp, she thought as she felt for Grayson's belt buckle. If he wasn't going to worry about it, then neither would she. Drawing in a ragged breath, she slipped her hands below his waistband. He was hard and ready for her.

Tessa's entire body vibrated with need. Specifically, the need for him to take her hard and fast. Anything slower or gentler would just be patronizing. She was done with him thinking of her as some sort of delicate flower that needed coddling.

Grayson captured one of her calves and pulled it away from his waist just long enough to unzip her boot and yank it off. The other one followed and, in a matter of seconds, his wide palms were skimming both her jeans and panties off her hips, sending them sliding down her thighs.

He withdrew something from his back pocket right before she pushed his jeans down lower. She heard the tearing of the foil packet. Grayson reached between them to sheath his length in a condom then positioned himself at her entrance. A tremor started deep inside Tessa's core and she was afraid she would lose herself before they'd even started.

His teeth grazed the lobe of her ear as he asked, "You ready for this?"

"Please don't stop now," she told him and linked her ankles behind his back.

Grayson entered her swiftly and she gasped, shuddering from the fullness of him. He dipped his hips lower, adjusting his angle, and joined their bodies together again and again. She didn't know where her breathing started and where his ended. The marbled entryway echoed every moan and whimper and sigh. Each thrust brought him deeper, brought them closer.

His breath was hot and fast against her cheek. His skin smelled of soap and eucalyptus, and she traced her lips along his jawline and back to his mouth, the whiskers of his five-o'clock shadow making her tingle even more. He captured her tongue once again and dug his fingers into the curve of her hips, holding her in place as he brought her to the highest peak.

He let out a final groan as he shuddered, his release coming right after hers. When the aftershocks faded, Tessa felt the rise and fall of his chest against hers. Their heart rates returned to a normal pace and he buried his mouth against the softest part of her neck.

Tessa didn't think it was possible, but Grayson lifted her even closer to him. He held her tightly as he walked toward the bed. When he lay down next to her on the white sheets, his finger started a trail at her collarbone, moving between her breasts and dipping below her belly button.

She shivered then offered him a satisfied smile. "Now what?"

"Now—" he moved over her "—I'm going to take my time."

Grayson caught sight of a bruise on Tessa's right hip as she stretched in bed early the following morning. Wincing, he asked, "Did I do that?"

"I hope so." She smiled at him. Her eyes glanced at the bedside clock and she gave him a sly grin. "Do you have time before your shift starts to kiss it and make it better?"

Growling, his hand snaked around her waist and he pulled her to him. But before they could start another round of lovemaking, her smartphone vibrated on the nightstand with an incoming call. He tried to ignore it, but then there were a series of pings as the screen lit up with several notification bubbles.

Tessa sighed. "I should probably get that."

She stretched across him to reach for her phone and he took the opportunity to playfully lick the pink nipple poised directly over his head. Unfortunately, her groan wasn't one of pleasure.

He scooted out from underneath her and saw that her face had lost some color. "What's wrong?"

Instead of replying, she showed him her phone screen and his stomach sank. The image on the screen showed Grayson and Tessa clinging to each other in a passionate kiss. In the picture, he could make out the rows of liquor bottles behind them, the green knit cap sitting on the bar beside Tessa.

He didn't bother asking the question he already knew the answer to. The photo could only have been taken last night, when they'd been so engrossed in each other, he hadn't thought about anything else. Grayson sagged against the upholstered headboard, resting his elbows on his knees as he rubbed at his face and dragged his hands through his hair.

He breathed in through his nose several times as he struggled to bring his frustration under control. When he finally raised his head, Tessa was staring off into the distance. He put his hand under her chin and forced her to look at him. "I'm sorry, Tess. I should've had better situational awareness. I knew the huge windows were a risk and I let my guard down."

Instead of berating him—like she had the first time they'd met—she smoothed his hair off his forehead. "You weren't on duty, remember? It wasn't your responsibility to protect me or my reputation last night. Besides, it's not like anyone could really confirm it's us."

The tiniest flicker of hope spiked through his chest, even as he lowered an eyebrow in doubt.

"Look." She held up the phone again. "It only

shows the sides of our faces and they're all smooshed together..."

Her voice trailed off as her thumb swiped the screen and another image appeared. This time, it was a picture of them turned toward each other, not quite kissing, so their profiles were easier to identify. She swiped again and there they were, facing the camera—wherever it had been hiding—and holding hands as they exited the bar. In the third shot, there was absolutely no question that the people in the photo were Grayson and Tessa.

Damn. His fist clenched the pillow as he fought the urge to throw something across the room. Instead of succumbing to his mounting frustration, he slipped the phone from her hand and brought it closer so he could read the article underneath. His eyes landed on phrases like "bodyguard for hire" and "boy toy" and "Davis Townsend's replacement."

But the worst part of the article was the last paragraph where it listed his name and what exactly he did for the Secret Service, including his office location and team assignment. There was even a picture of Grayson in full tactical gear with several other agents when he'd been on the counter assault team a few years ago.

He was no longer the mysterious Agent Steamy, he realized as his blood ran cold. Not only had his cover been blown, his entire career had been turned into tabloid fodder. It would only be a matter of time until the press got wind of Maddie and started showing up at her hospital.

"How do you deal with this all the time?" he asked, unable to hide the disgust in his voice.

"Deal with what? The complete lack of privacy?" Tessa shrugged, taking her phone back. "I grew up with it. My dad was in high-profile politics before I was even born. Being surrounded by cameras constantly is a tough lifestyle, but it's all I've ever known."

"Most of your siblings could say the same thing. Yet you're the only King who sought a career in the limelight."

"I didn't seek it." Tessa pulled the sheet up over her naked breasts and lifted her chin. "I majored in political science because it was a way to understand my father better, to understand the thing he loved as much as his family. It turned from researching to analyzing and, eventually, my dad coming to me for advice. I'd had a front-row seat to government in action my whole life and I was good at asking the right questions and digging for answers. The cameras were there long before I came along. I just learned how to do what I was good at while they were already rolling."

"Remember that time you commented on how I never seemed to be off duty?" he asked then waited for her stiff nod before continuing. "Well, when does Tessa King ever get a break to just be herself? Don't you ever get tired of constantly being on display for the world to see? With always having to fall in line with the public's perception of you whether you agree with it or not?"

Tessa's spine straightened. "Grayson, this is my life. My career. Yes, I chose it. And I'd choose it again because I'm doing a job that I love. A job that I think actually matters. People deserve to have a free press and access to global information. Not all journalists and reporters are like these guys." She pointed to the name of the online gossip rag on her screen.

"I get that. But it's nobody's business whether or not *'Beautiful Heiress Tessa King Slips Off to Love Nest with Sexy Bodyguard,'*" he quoted the headline. "I never asked for this kind of notoriety."

"Grayson, I never intended for you to be the subject of unwanted fame and attention. I don't blame you for being upset. But at the end of the day, this is what my job entails. I want you in my life. However, if you want to have any sort of relationship with me, then this is part of the package."

Grayson tried to latch onto the words he'd wanted to hear since he'd left the Twin Kings Ranch. Tessa King wanted him in her life. The bond they shared was way more than just a physical attraction.

Instead of euphoria, though, it was a bittersweetness that hung in the air between them. Because no matter how much they might want to be together, there was too much keeping them apart.

"Of course I want to have a relationship with you, Tessa." Grayson climbed out of the bed and looked around the hotel room floor for his discarded pants. "I don't want to have to sneak around to have one, either. When we were on the ranch, I fell for you harder than I could've imagined. The problem is that *my* job, *my* life, demands discretion. I'm trained to stay in the shadows and not draw any attention to the people I'm protecting. I can't do my job if the paparazzi are constantly dogging me or flashing my picture all over the internet."

He was also trained to retreat and reformulate a plan once he determined what he was up against. Or maybe this was it. The battle was over and it was time to admit defeat and tend to his wounds.

Grayson finally found his jeans on the marble floor in the entryway. Right next to the upended lamp he'd knocked over when he'd made love to Tessa before they could reach the bed. The memory flooded through him, taking some of the sting out of his disappointment. He yanked his jeans into place, trying not to think of her breathy little pants last night as she'd begged him for more.

Tessa appeared in the entryway behind him, her messy blond curls framing her proud face. She'd kept the sheet wrapped around her torso, but her swollen lips were turned down at the corners.

"When I met you at the bar last night, I'd hoped for a better ending than this," she offered. "I fell for you just as hard. Literally. I'd tried to stay away this past month to give us space so we could figure out who we were outside of the ranch, and what we both wanted. But it looks like this is how things have to be if we both want to keep doing what we're made to do. I'm sorry, Grayson."

"I know." He exhaled. "I'm sorry, too."

She didn't tell him to stay. She didn't tell him that they could work through this together. Most important, she didn't ask him to give up his job or anything else to be with her.

In that moment, Grayson loved her even more.

His phone pinged from inside his jacket pocket, where he'd left it last night. He pulled it out to see an incoming message from SAIC Simon. Just when Grayson thought his heart couldn't take any more blows, another round breached his walls.

"Listen. I've got to go to work." He didn't add that Simon had just informed him he was officially off protective detail now that his temporary celebrity status could compromise the assignment. He didn't want Tessa to blame herself.

Twelve hours ago, he'd never expected them to ride into the sunset together. So then why did it suddenly feel as though he was leaving part of himself behind? Grayson's insides twisted with remorse knowing that this was the end of the road for them. Things had ended almost as quickly as they had begun.

The longing for her, though, would likely never go away.

Tessa stood there, the sheet clasped around her, her shoulders back and her chin high. She may be disappointed, but she wouldn't admit it. Tessa King would dive into another new project in no time.

Before he walked out the door, he gave her cheek one last caress and whispered, "Take care of yourself."

Chapter Thirteen

"No, I haven't heard from him in over three days," Tessa told Aunt Freckles the following Saturday afternoon via video chat from the comfort of the sleek leather sofa inside her Georgetown town house. Freckles must have set her smartphone on the counter while she poured batter into cupcake cups because Tessa could see most of the Twin Kings' kitchen in the background.

She was surprised at the pang of wistfulness for her childhood home. Perhaps it had to do with the fact that everyone in her family was busy today prepping for a birthday party for Marcus's twins. After spending so much time in Wyoming recently, Tessa suddenly felt as though she was missing out on something.

"So he split, just like that, huh?" Freckles called out over her shoulder as she slid a tray of cupcakes into the oven. "Do you know if he's still in Philadelphia?"

Tessa shook her head. "At least, I don't think so. I ran into Agent Doherty in the Ritz lobby the day after we, uh, had drinks." She certainly wasn't going to give her aunt too many details and risk Freckles wanting to return the favor by offering up details of her and Uncle Rider's bedroom time. Tessa shuddered before continuing. "Doherty said Grayson was transferred from the assignment. He didn't say where, and I was too embarrassed to ask."

"What do you have to be embarrassed about?" Freckles asked as she returned to her mixing bowl, which must have been where the phone was propped because all Tessa could see was a close-up view of the Cowgirl Up Café logo across the woman's too tight T-shirt.

Tessa blinked several times before deciding it was easier to focus on the cherry blossom trees outside her window than on her senior citizen aunt's substantial bosom. "Because it was being with me that cost Grayson his job. Or at least his job in the Protective Intelligence Division."

"Darlin', don't you ever apologize for being a woman in the prime of your life. You have physical needs. Heck, we all do." Freckles added with a chuckle, "It's why I keep letting your uncle Rider talk me into staying at his cabin every night."

This was the exact visual Tessa had been trying to avoid. But how could she fault anyone for sharing too much information about their love life? Half the world had seen that intimate picture of Tessa and Grayson making out in some dive bar in Philadelphia.

"Now, I know sometimes men don't always think with the head upstairs." Freckles used a measuring spoon to point at her helmet of orangish-colored curls. "But, from what I saw, that Agent Wyatt is a planner. One of those fellas that calculates risks and strategies and keeps an eye out for hidden land mines. You never pretended to be anyone other than yourself. He knew exactly what he was getting into from the moment he first met you."

Tessa let the words settle over her. "Maybe that's why he seemed to already have his exit strategy in place."

"Then again…" Freckles tsked as she returned to the center island to pour out another batch. "Fame's not for everyone, darlin'. I couldn't wait to leave it all behind the second I turned eighteen. The day after my debutante ball, I hauled butt outta Boston so fast, those Beacon Hill society matrons' heads were spinning."

"I know." Tessa frowned, trying to figure out if

her aunt was on her side or his. Freckles could play a mean devil's advocate. "I don't blame Grayson for not wanting to be a part of all that. Deep inside, I think we both knew that anything serious between us wouldn't have worked in the long run. I guess I was just hoping things could've lasted a little longer."

"If I've learned a little something from my seventy-plus years on this earth, it's how to deal with heartbreak."

"Seventy-plus years?" Tessa's mother glided into the kitchen just then and stopped at the specialty blender on the counter behind Freckles. "More like eighty-plus years."

Freckles flicked some of the flour off her hands and the white powder clung to the back of Sherilee's bright cashmere sweater.

Tessa rolled her eyes at the two women. Maybe she didn't miss home as much as she'd first thought. Normally, she would've called Duke for advice, but he was on a classified assignment.

"I'm not suffering from anything as serious as heartbreak, Aunt Freckles," Tessa said, knowing full well it was a lie. If she hadn't already been half in love with Grayson when he'd been on that diving board with her, then it would've happened when he'd done the gentlemanly thing and given her the space to figure out her feelings on her own.

"When you think about the man, does your rib cage get all tight? Do you spend so much time thinking about what he might be doing that when you walk into a room, you forget why you went in there in the first place?" The loose skin on Freckles's neck wobbled as she nodded knowingly. "If so, it's definitely a broken heart."

"It could also be another panic attack." Her mom dropped a bag of fresh kale as she rushed over to the smartphone screen. "Have you seen your neurologist yet, Contessa?"

"It's not a panic attack, Mom. Or heartbreak. It's just..." An empty feeling, Tessa thought. A feeling of jumping off a high dive and expecting to hit the water but just free-falling into air. She bit back the words to keep from saying as much out loud. "I don't know what it is."

"Uh-oh." Sherilee narrowed her eyes as though she could study Tessa's emotions through the screen. "You don't know what it is because you've never felt it before. I experienced the same thing when I fell head-over-heels for your father. I was young. I'd never been in love before. I thought I had my life all planned out in my mind. Then Roper King showed up and turned my whole world upside down. One minute I was telling myself all the reasons why this older guy with a campaign bus full of baggage was all wrong for me and the next I couldn't imagine spending my life without him."

Tessa didn't like how eerily similar her mother's past experience was sounding to her own. She shook off the feeling. "In this situation, though, I *have* to imagine my life without Grayson. His job and mine just aren't compatible and neither one of us could ask the other to give up so much. Unlike you and Dad, it's just not meant to be."

"Not meant to be?" Sherilee King asked. "You're talking to a girl who went from the trailer park to the Twin Kings to the White House. You think being married to Roper King was a walk in the park? He was a recovering alcoholic and I was a cocktail waitress and half his age. Talk about incompatible lives. You should've heard what the press used to say when we'd show up at an event. But we didn't let that stop us. We didn't throw up our hands in the air and say it wasn't meant to be."

"Wait. You were a cocktail waitress?" Of all the things her mother had just shared, Tessa wasn't sure why she'd narrowed in on that one tiny detail. Maybe it was because of Sherilee's well-known disapproval of Dahlia running Big Millie's. "Dad met you in a bar?"

"He'd fallen off the wagon, so to speak, and I helped him get back on. So contrary to popular belief," her mother gave a pointed look at Aunt Freckles, "it was me who rescued him first. Not the other way around."

"Wow. I never knew that." Tessa let out the breath she hadn't known she'd been holding. "Clearly, Dad wanted to be rescued. And lucky for all of us that he did."

"But?" her mom prompted.

"But, I don't think that's the case with Grayson. He likes his life the way it is."

Sherilee brought the phone so close to her face, Tessa could practically see the hidden incisions of last year's eye lift. "If his job's an obstacle, I could always have a word with the director. He won't ever have to know."

"Oh my gosh, Mom! You sound like a mob boss. I don't want you to have Grayson fired."

"How about we just get him reassigned to something more manageable? Maybe he'd like a desk job once he got used to it. The commissioner over at the Internal Revenue Service owes me a favor…"

"Mom! Stop! You can't fix this. I have to let Grayson go."

"But what if…"

"The best way to get over a man—" Freckles's bright fingernails flashed on the screen before she wrestled the smartphone out of Sherilee's grip "—is to learn and grow from the relationship, no matter how brief it might've been."

"Well, you'd be the one to know, seeing as how you're the queen of brief relationships," Tessa's mother muttered to her aunt.

Freckles thankfully refused to take the bait. "Listen, darlin'. What you need to do is find something good that came out of the affair. What did you learn from it? How are you a better person from it?"

"Or you can always throw yourself into charity." Her mom stuck a spoon into a bowl of chocolate frosting. "That's what I always do to get my mind off things."

Mom shoved the spoon in her mouth quickly, but Freckles had eyes in the back of her head. "Then why don't you go volunteer somewhere, Sherilee, instead of stress eating all my food before this afternoon's party?"

"Because my kids all need me here right now." Her mother continued to list every single cause for stress—no matter how insignificant—currently occurring on Twin Kings Ranch. Each one involved one of Tessa's siblings and whomever they may or may not be dating.

By the time Tessa disconnected the call, she suddenly wished she had her own tray of cupcakes to shovel down her mouth. She walked to the kitchen, wanting to dive into a meal or something else that would take her mind off her heartbreak. *Disappointment*, she quickly corrected herself, wishing her aunt had never used the *H* word.

But the only food in her refrigerator was a three-day-old chicken-and-pesto wrap from the craft services table at work, and half a jar of green olives. Tessa decided to avoid the risk of any lurking photographers camping out in front of the gourmet market down the street and placed an online order for grocery delivery.

Shopping for dinner on an empty stomach had been a mistake, though, she later realized when all the items in her virtual shopping cart totaled over five hundred dollars and couldn't be delivered for almost three hours. Instead of waiting patiently for her groceries, she called her favorite Thai take-out place and the manager promised to have her order of coconut chicken soup and drunken noodles at her front door in less than thirty minutes.

With dinner on its way, Tessa was left to ponder how she could grow from her extremely short-lived relationship with Grayson. She returned to her laptop and tapped absently at the mouse. What did she learn from Agent Wyatt? Other than that little trick he did with his tongue when he…

Focus, she commanded her brain. Opening the internet home page, she tried scrolling through her search history. She really needed to clean out her web browser, she concluded as she looked at everything she'd researched in the past few months. There had to be something in here that might trigger an idea.

She was still tapping at the down arrow when her eyes landed on it.

EDMD.

Maddie's medical condition. Tessa had asked Grayson about his sister at some point during the evening when they'd slept together. He'd told her that Maddie's procedure was showing some signs of progress and allowing her more movement. He'd tamped down Tessa's excitement by reminding her that Maddie would never regain the full use of her muscles. But even Grayson couldn't hide the twinkle of hope when he'd added, "The good news is that the doctors think she might be able to eventually get back on a horse one day."

His words about getting back on a horse replayed in Tessa's mind as she ate her Thai food and researched equestrian therapy opportunities. By the end of the night, she'd scribbled down a slew of notes and had the perfect idea on how to implement both Freckles's and her mother's advice at the same time.

Tessa would use what she'd learned from her relationship with Grayson to make someone else's world a better place.

Grayson hadn't seen Tessa in almost a month—in person at least. He'd caught a glimpse of her on a television set in the lobby of the hospital when he'd been waiting for Maddie to be discharged a couple of weeks ago. Then again last Tuesday when she'd been on location in the Midwest, discussing the aftermath of a multivortex tornado that had left the residents of a poorer community without electricity and running water while a neighboring county with a higher tax revenue had its power restored immediately.

Seeing her on the screen each time made his lungs

seize midbreath, as though someone had sucker punched him in the solar plexus. If it was painful enough for him to watch her from hundreds of miles away, he didn't want to think about how painful it would be if he saw her in person.

When the inquiry board had concluded its investigation and he'd been cleared to return to his team, Grayson had expected to feel a sense of relief. A sense of closure where Tessa King had been concerned. But then an instructor at the James J. Rowley Training Center referenced the funeral incident involving Tessa as a case study in tactical emergencies, and asked Grayson to speak to a class of recruits about unusual protective detail scenarios.

The presentation and subsequent role-playing drills during Grayson's crisis training simulations went so well, the director at the JJRTC invited him to formally transfer to Maryland and become a permanent instructor. The change in assignment was not only closer to his family in Baltimore, it meant that news vans had less access to him on the enclosed five-hundred-acre facility.

While he'd always preferred being in the role of operative—the guy who comes in and gets the job done—he had to be totally honest. Ever since that night on the diving board with Tessa, Grayson had gotten a taste for inspiring others. Now he looked forward to the challenges of training the up-and-coming agents.

Plus, the new assignment came along with his pick of challenging physical endurance courses, firing ranges and bomb detection simulations whenever he needed an adrenaline fix. Intense tactical training and hand-to-hand combat beat a boring six-mile jog any day of the week.

Grayson's phone vibrated against his belt right as he finished his workout on the rope course with the Spec Ops team. He was still catching his breath when he swiped his thumb across the screen to answer.

"Hey, Mads. How was pool therapy today?"

"Forget about pool therapy, Grayson." His sister's words came out in a rush. "Have you seen the pledge drive?"

"What pledge drive?" he asked, digging into his duffel bag for his stainless steel canteen.

"The one Tessa King launched last night on her show. Didn't you watch?"

Grayson almost choked on his gulp of water. He cleared his throat and then unclipped himself from his harness. He didn't tell his kid sister that watching his ex—did Tessa even qualify as an ex if they'd only spent one night together?—made him feel as though a hiking carabiner was clamped around his heart.

"Nah, I missed it."

"Well, she did an hour-long special about neurological disabilities and the need for physical therapy facilities outside of doctors' offices. Grayson, remember that horse camp I went to when we were teens?" Maddie didn't give him a chance to answer. "She had the owner of Let's Ride on her show talking about how it's not just kids that need to be on horseback, or zip-lining through the trees, or rowing across lakes or any of other things that get people rehabbing in the fresh air. And she's right. I mean, it's great for the kids, of course. And I'm all for her raising money for camps like that. But those kids are going to grow up someday, hopefully, and then where do they go? No more fancy unconventional rehab programs for them. No more horses or aquatic centers unless they have the money to pay for them out of pocket."

"Slow down," Grayson told his sister, but should've told his own mind because his head was already spinning. "You're saying Tessa King is trying to raise money for adults with physical limitations to go to horse camps?"

"Not trying to, Grayson. She already did. After only twenty-four hours, the fund she started, called— get this—the Coach Oliver Foundation, has already raised twelve million dollars. She's also lobbying for more insurance companies to cover alternative forms of physical therapy."

He stood motionless as the information sank in. All of the football players at Montgomery High had loved Coach Oliver Wyatt. He'd never told Tessa anything about his father, yet somehow she'd found out and named the foundation after a man she hadn't even met. Grayson's heart went from being squeezed to being in danger of flying out of his chest.

Maddie kept talking and it took Grayson a few seconds to catch up to what his sister had just said. "What did you just say about sweeps week?"

"I said that every other station and newspaper is reporting nonstop about that scandal with General What's-His-Name. But Tessa waited for the peak week during the Nielsen sweeps, when TV ratings are at an all-time high, to use her time on the air to help people like our family. See, Grayson. Not everyone in the media is a vulture out to pick your bones clean."

Grayson chugged more water, as if he could refill the sudden emptiness churning inside. "When did I ever tell you that?"

"The day before the doctors released me. Mom had just seen that article with you and Tessa King kissing in some magazine she'd found in the hospital cafeteria. She asked you if you were actually dating Tessa and you told her not to believe everything she read in the news. Then she told you a picture was worth a thousand words and—"

"I remember," he interrupted before she could get to the part where their mom warned him that being in the spotlight was preferable to him living in the shadows. "I thought you'd been asleep when she brought that up."

"You guys always have the best conversations

when you think I'm sleeping. Like that time you told her that you were enlisting in the military instead of going straight to college, and she told you that Daddy would've wanted you to finish your education. Or that time when you told her that you and Jamie were getting divorced, and she told you that someday the right woman would come along and you'd realize that there was so much more to life than sacrificing yourself to the overtime gods."

Grayson's stomach was now full of both water and guilt. He tossed his empty canteen back inside his bag. "Did you also overhear us the time we were talking about you no longer watching those true crime documentaries because you were the worst detective ever?"

"Nah, I must've been sleeping for real during *that* conversation." Maddie laughed. "Hey, I gotta go. I have an online class starting in two minutes. But make sure you check out the website for the Coach Oliver Foundation."

They disconnected and Grayson hauled his gear and rucksack across the sprawling campus to the dorm rooms where some of the instructors stayed during the week. He couldn't remember the last time he'd slept in a bed that he actually owned.

His mom and Maddie had downsized to a smaller, inexpensive apartment when he'd joined the Marines. Grayson'd had a handful of furnished rental units here and there, including the six months he and Jamie had lived overseas. But he'd lived most of his adult life out of barracks, hotel rooms and bunkhouses.

As he let himself into the dorm and appraised the cheap blue comforter, along with the basic dresser and matching desk, a vision of the main house at the Twin Kings Ranch popped into his head. What would it feel like to actually live in a real home? Not one that expensive or vast, obviously. But one that had been built and decorated specifically for his tastes. One that had Tessa relaxing inside after they'd both come home from a fulfilling day at work.

Grayson took a quick shower—at least these temporary accommodations had a private bathroom— then powered on his laptop. He had a few minutes before teaching his next class and should've spent the time researching apartments in the nearby town of Laurel, Maryland.

Instead, he found himself scrolling through the Coach Oliver Foundation's website. The digital counter on the bottom of the screen kept changing numbers as donations poured in by the minute. Even though he'd once lumped Tessa into the same boat as tabloid reporters on the prowl for a sensationalized story, deep down he'd known she'd always used her media platform for good. Whether it was bringing awareness to those in need, or exposing corporate and government corruption, or interrogating some of the most powerful people in the world, she didn't back down from a challenge. Just like her diving, she did everything thoroughly and with exacting precision.

She also didn't invest herself in a matter unless it was important to her. All this time, Grayson had been so preoccupied thinking about that video recording of her in the staging center tent, and worrying about her throwing him under the bus, he hadn't realized he'd been doing exactly the same thing to her when he'd left her like that.

Tessa was one of the few people who knew that Maddie's care was a top priority in his life. Instead of cutting all ties with him when he'd told her he couldn't date someone with her level of fame, she'd spun that fame to *his* advantage. Or, at least, to his sister's.

That had to mean she still cared about him, right? And maybe if she still cared, there was a chance he could convince her that he'd made the biggest mistake of his life when he'd walked out of the hotel room. Grayson wasn't convinced she'd forgive him, but for the first time in weeks, he was also full of hope.

There was no way to know if Tessa would even consider the possibility of a partnership again after he'd already refused to go into battle with her once. All Grayson knew was that the most successful missions required an advance plan. He picked up his phone and called the only person he knew with a special forces background and a working knowledge of seeking forgiveness from a female in the King family.

When Rider King answered, Grayson cleared his throat.

"Hello, sir. I was wondering if I could talk with you about Tessa."

Chapter Fourteen

Grayson never should have listened to the wily old rancher, he thought as he led his class of recruits across the South Lawn of the White House. The chairs had already been placed in the Rose Garden for an informal awards ceremony, and his students were in attendance merely for observational purposes.

Somehow, Rider King had talked Grayson into convincing his director and the director of the protective detail assigned to the White House that the recruits needed practical, real world application of their training in the most boring of circumstances.

It just so happened that the boring circumstance

Grayson deemed most suitable for the training was one in which former Second Lady Sherilee King was to be awarded the Presidential Medal of Freedom in recognition of her contributions to philanthropy.

Not that anything was all that boring when the entire King family came together.

Briefing all the agents on duty and the president's chief of staff had been one of the most awkward presentations Grayson had ever endured. But if things went according to plan, nobody would know the real reason he'd staged such an unbelievable scenario.

"Precision has landed," Grayson heard in his earpiece as he herded the recruits to the observation area. That meant Tessa was on the premises. But they still had a few minutes before everyone took their seats. It wasn't until he saw the news cameras setting up that Grayson realized there'd be no going back after this.

He spotted Rider King near some foliage outside the west colonnade, the gray felt Stetson he wore for "fancy occasions" making him stand out above everyone else. Grayson strode over to the older man and asked, "Sir, are you sure this will work?"

"Not if Freckles catches me out here, it won't." Rider held out a circular tin of chewing tobacco to Grayson. "Want a dip?"

"I don't mean sneaking out here for a wad of chew." Grayson tried to ignore the pounding in his temples. "I meant this plan today with me and Tessa."

"Considerin' you haven't found any other way to get her attention..." the old man started then shrugged. "I don't see how it could hurt your chances none."

"But won't Mrs. King be upset that we're upstaging her award ceremony?"

"It was Sherilee who thought of this idea in the first place, son. I'm just a good soldier who does what I'm told."

"Oh hell." Grayson looked upward, hoping a freak thunderstorm would engulf him. But the April sky was a clear blue.

Mrs. King walked up at just that moment and used her little purse to swat the container out of her brother-in-law's hand. "Rider King, you know full well that tobacco products aren't allowed on government property."

Rider jumped back. "Damn it, woman, I thought you were Freckles. That sounded exactly like the kinda thing she would say."

Mrs. King's eyes darted back and forth between him and the half-empty tin. She sighed. "Carry on, then."

Grayson wanted to commend the older man on his well-played reverse psychology, but Tessa's mother turned her attention to him instead. "It looks like all the camera crews are in position. Are you ready?"

"I'm ready, ma'am. However, I do have just a few concerns about the execution of this particular strategy."

Mrs. King gave him a chilling look. "You changed your mind about Tessa?"

"No, it's not that at all. I love your daughter, ma'am, and I wouldn't be here right now if I didn't want to be with her." Grayson waited for Mrs. King's pursed mouth to relax before he continued. "Remember when Davis Townsend came out to the ranch to propose to Tessa? Wasn't that your idea, too?"

"Of course it was."

"Well, that didn't work out so well. Why would this time be any different?"

Mrs. King rolled her eyes. "What are you talking about? Davis did exactly what I wanted him to do and Tessa reacted exactly as I'd expected. She'd been dragging that breakup on for way too long and sometimes we just need to rip the Band-Aid off, if you know what I'm saying."

"So you knew she'd break up with him?" he asked, bewildered.

Mrs. King's sigh was one of exasperation. "Obviously. The trick was getting Townsend to bring his press secretary along. Tessa doesn't mind the cameras when it's for work. But she hates all that extra publicity just to show off."

"But then why are we…" Grayson started and Mrs. King swatted at the air, dismissing his confusion as if it was an annoying fly.

"If Davis had truly cared about my daughter, he would've foregone the cameras and kept things private. But he wasn't willing to step outside his comfort zone for her. But you, Agent Wyatt? You're willing to make a real sacrifice. That's the ultimate gesture." Mrs. King looped her arm through Rider's. "Now, let's all get into position."

Grayson looked toward the sky again, wondering if there had in fact been a thunderstorm, because Mrs. King's reasoning left him in a fall-out shelter of confusion.

He should have been comforted by the woman's faith in him and this plan. But no other mission had been as important to him as this one.

He couldn't lose Tessa for good.

"And none of this would have been possible if I didn't have the loving support of my family behind me," Tessa's mother said into the eight microphones affixed to the podium. Shutters clicked all around them, and Tessa fought the urge to look around at the Secret Service agents hovering in the background to see if any of them might be Grayson.

But he was long gone and her plan to get over him by diving into a charitable endeavor had backfired. Planning the fundraiser with Maddie and Mrs. Wyatt only made Tessa miss Grayson all the more.

"Come on up here, kids," her mom said, and Uncle Rider gave Tessa a nudge.

What? This wasn't part of the plan. The president was supposed to award her mom the medal, her mom was supposed to give a brief speech, and then they were supposed to meet in the West Wing reception area for light refreshments and some informal pictures. Nobody was supposed to be called onstage.

Tessa's eyes shot to Marcus who was already halfway to the podium with a sullen MJ in tow. Next, she looked at Dahlia and Finn, who were both refusing to make eye contact with her as they took turns pushing one another to the front of the pack. She finally got Duke's attention.

"What's going on?" Tessa asked under her breath as they joined their siblings. "Mom never goes off script."

"Remember what Dad said the first time he taught you how to jump into an eddy in the Snake River?" Duke replied, but the crowd was clapping politely and he had to pause so that he could smile and wave to the cameras aimed in their direction. Her brother glanced at something behind Tessa and then finished, "Just tuck your knees up and roll with it."

Tessa barely had time to process his words when she felt herself being lifted into the air. An *oomph* escaped her lips as she bounced against a solid chest. Then she saw who that chest belonged to and all the air left her body.

"This gets easier every time I do it," Grayson said into her ear as he turned toward the wall of lenses zooming in on them. He cradled her in his arms as reporters yelled out questions, but the only thing she could hear right that second was her pounding heart. And him. "But I have no problem practicing it over and over again until I get it right."

"What are you doing here?" Tessa tilted her head as she looked between Grayson's face and the entire press corps assigned to the White House. She tentatively wrapped her arms around his shoulders for balance.

"Well, I thought I could go back to my own life and you could go back to yours. But I was absolutely lost without you," he said, and Tessa was glad he was holding her because her legs would've turned to jelly. "So, I'm making another daring rescue. Except this time, I'm rescuing myself."

Another wave of shuttering cameras peppered the air and she lifted her brow. "Isn't this the part where you usually sprint us off to safety?"

"I want them to look their fill and take as many pictures as they need." Then Grayson kissed her, right there in front of her family, and the president and the entire world watching from home. When he finally pulled back, he stared into her eyes as though they were the only two people there. "I love you, Tessa King, and that's not something I ever want to keep to myself again."

Tessa's chest couldn't contain all the pounding and excitement racing through her heart. She'd known that he cared for her, but she hadn't thought he'd be willing to give up everything else in his life for her. "But what about your job?"

"I transferred to the JJRTC to become an instructor. Apparently, the recruits seem to think that my unfounded celebrity status somehow means I actually know what I'm teaching them."

"And the notoriety?" She bit her lower lip.

He hefted her closer to him. "You told me that being with you meant that I had to accept being in the spotlight. It'll be a learning curve for me, and I can't always promise that I'll do or say the right things when the cameras are rolling. But I'd rather be by your side than anywhere else in the world. This is my way of proving it to you."

Tessa pulled his face to hers and kissed him again. "I love you, too, Grayson. I promise to hold on to you this time, to be *your* protector and to try to shield you whenever I can. If things ever get too overwhelming, we can always go hide out at the ranch."

Just when she thought her heart was going to burst, her family closed ranks around them, making the moment even more special because they were all a part of it.

Uncle Rider tugged his cowboy hat lower on his head and asked, "So, who planned the exit strategy?"

"Well, you guys told me I couldn't bring the horses." Finn threw her arms up. "So I thought someone else was planning it."

"Don't look at me." MJ shoved his hands into his

pockets. "Sheriff Big Brother over there is still holding my driver's license hostage."

Everyone began speaking at once and, as her family argued among themselves, Tessa asked Grayson, "Are you sure you know what you signed up for?"

"Not really. When it comes to you and your family, I'm finding that all my rules and careful strategizing can easily be blown off course. You're the only assignment I want, though, so it looks like I'll just have to hold steady."

"Then let's get out of here." Tessa smiled at him before giving him another kiss.

Grayson walked her through the Rose Garden, over the South Lawn and toward the Ellipse. "I didn't want to leave any of the planning to your family, so I took the liberty of securing a transport vehicle for our dramatic exit."

She narrowed her eyes. "I love you, Agent Wyatt, but there's no way I'm getting into another hearse with you."

He barked out a laugh and she felt his chest vibrate against her.

"Don't worry." Grayson nodded toward the helipad. She turned to see the small green helicopter with the Buster Chop's Chopper Rentals logo on the tail. "I got the next best thing."

* * * * *

Look for Dahlia's story,
Making Room for the Rancher
by Christy Jeffries

The next installment in her new miniseries,
Twin Kings Ranch,
On sale March 2021

Wherever Harlequin Books and ebooks are sold.

COMING NEXT MONTH FROM

⊕ HARLEQUIN

SPECIAL EDITION

Available January 26, 2021

#2815 WYOMING CINDERELLA
Dawson Family Ranch • by Melissa Senate

Molly Orton has loved Zeke Dawson since middle school. And now the scrappy single mom is ready to make her move. Except Zeke wants Molly to set him up with her knockout best friend! Molly knows if Zeke spends more time with her and her adorable baby, he'll see what love *really* looks like. All this plain Jane needs is a little Cinderella magic...

#2816 THEIR SECOND-TIME VALENTINE
The Fortunes of Texas: The Hotel Fortune • by Helen Lacey

Kane Fortune has never had any trouble attracting women—he's just never been the type to stick around. Until he meets widowed mom Layla McCarthy and her adorable toddler. But Layla's worried he's not up to the job of *lifetime* valentine. Kane will have his work cut out for him proving he's right for the role.

#2817 THE HOME THEY BUILT
Blackberry Bay • by Shannon Stacey

Host Anna Beckett knows clear well the Weaver house has never been a functioning inn, but taking the project got her to Blackberry Bay...the only place she'll ever find answers about her own family. Will her secrets threaten the budding romance between her and fake handyman Finn Weaver?

#2818 THE COWGIRL'S SURPRISE MATCH
Tillbridge Stables • by Nina Crespo

To keep the secret wedding plans from leaking to the press, Zurie Tillbridge and Mace Calderone must pretend *they* are the ones getting married. Cake tasting and flower arranging seem like harmless fun...until wary workaholic Zurie realizes she's feeling something real for her fake fiancé...

#2819 A SECRET BETWEEN US
Rancho Esperanza • by Judy Duarte

Pregnant waitress Callie Jamison was settling in to her new life in Fairborn, Montana, dividing her time between the ranch and the diner...and Ramon Cruz, the sexy town councilman, who never fails to show up for the breakfast shift. But will he still feel the same when he learns the secret Callie has been keeping?

#2820 HER MOUNTAINSIDE HAVEN
Gallant Lake Stories • by Jo McNally

Jillie Coleman has created a carefully constructed world for herself, complete with therapy dog Sophie, top-of-the-line security systems and a no-neighbors policy at her mountaintop retreat. But when intriguing developer Matt Danzer shows up, planning to develop the abandoned ski resort on the other side of the mountain, Jillie finds her stand-alone resolve starting to crumble...

HSECNM0121

*Jillie's a bestselling horror writer who wants to be left
alone in her isolated mountainside cabin. Matt bought
the abandoned ski resort next door and plans to reopen
it. These uneasy neighbors battle over everything...*

Read on for a sneak peek at
Her Mountainside Haven,
the next book in the Gallant Lake Stories
by Jo McNally.

"And your secluded mountainside home with the
fancy electronics is part of that safety net? And your
hellhound?"

Jillie chuckled, looking up to where Sophie was
glaring down at Matt from the deck. "Don't insult my
dog. She's more for companionship than protection.
Although her appearance doesn't hurt." She shuddered
and pulled her jacket tighter.

God, he'd kept her standing out here in the cold and
dark while he grilled her with questions. She'd already
hinted that it was time for him to go. He scrubbed his
hands down his face.

"I'm sorry, Jillie. You must be freezing. Go on up.
Once I know you're inside, I'll take off."

"And you were on your way to dinner. You must
be starving." She hesitated for just a moment. In that
moment, he *really* wanted her to invite him up to join

her for dinner, but that didn't happen. Instead, she flashed him a quick smile before turning to go. "Thanks again, Matt."

Let her walk away. Way too complicated. Just let her walk away.

She was all the way up to the deck when he heard his own voice calling out to her.

"The old ski lift is working well, but I need to give it a few test runs, just to get acquainted with the thing. If you want a ride up to that craggy summit you like so much, I'll be heading up there Sunday afternoon. It'll just be us. No workers. No spectators."

Her head started to move back and forth, then stopped. She looked down at him in silence, then gave a loud sigh. "Maybe. I'll let you know. I've…I've got to go in."

He watched her and Sophie go through the door. She turned and locked it, then gave him a stuttering wave. For someone obsessed with privacy, it was interesting that this entire wall, right up to the peak of the A-frame roof, was glass. He lifted his hand, then headed to his car. He wasn't sure what surprised him more. That he'd asked Jillie to ride to the top of the mountain with him, or that she'd said maybe. As he turned the ignition, he realized he was smiling.